# AN INTIMATE DANCE

After a very long time, when she was pleasantly dizzy and breathless, he slowed to a stop, but continued to hold her firmly against him. Prudence could feel the beating of his heart. She knew that hers was as rapid from the splendid exercise. She didn't want him to let go of her, and for a long time they remained locked in each other's arms. His breath whispered in her hair and she thought perhaps his lips brushed her temple.

Certainly his lips brushed her forehead now. And then they skimmed over her face, descending to her lips. His kiss was warm and gentle. But for all that, she could feel it tug at her. Prudence realized that the sensations in her body were becoming stronger. Her breasts, pressed against his chest, seemed to tingle. The tug at her core felt more like a yearning than like the bout of nerves she'd feared. Ledbetter's hands, rhythmic and soothing on her back, moved slightly lower. They spanned her waist and held her firmly against him. . . .

## *Coming next month*

### THE DUKE'S WAGER & LORD OF DISHONOR
#### by Edith Layton

For the first time, two Regency novels by acclaimed author Edith Layton—together in one volume!

**"One of the romance genre's greatest storytellers."**
— *Romantic Times*

0-451-20139-6/$5.50

### THE SELFLESS SISTER
#### by Shirley Kennedy

Lucinda Linley faces spinsterhood after putting her younger sisters' marriage prospects ahead of her own. Then she finds true love with the Lord of Ravensbrook—but will a long-standing family feud impede their future happiness?

**"Shirley Kennedy's Regencies are a delight."**
— *Debbie Macomber*

0-451-20138-8/$4.99

### THE MAJOR'S MISTAKE
#### by Andrea Pickens

Major Julian Miranda accepts a long-term army commission after catching his wife in what appears to be a very compromising position. Seven years later the couple meets again. But will it be pride—or passion—that wins the day?

0-451-20096-9/$4.99

# A Prudent Match

## Laura Matthews

A SIGNET BOOK

SIGNET
Published by New American Library, a division of
Penguin Putnam Inc., 375 Hudson Street,
New York, New York 10014, U.S.A.
Penguin Books Ltd, 27 Wrights Lane,
London W8 5TZ, England
Penguin Books Australia Ltd, Ringwood,
Victoria, Australia
Penguin Books Canada Ltd, 10 Alcorn Avenue,
Toronto, Ontario, Canada M4V 3B2
Penguin Books (N.Z.) Ltd, 182–190 Wairau Road,
Auckland 10, New Zealand

Penguin Books Ltd, Registered Offices:
Harmondsworth, Middlesex, England

First published by Signet, an imprint of New American Library,
a division of Penguin Putnam Inc.

First Printing, July 2000
10 9 8 7 6 5 4 3 2 1

PUBLISHER'S NOTE
This is a work of fiction. Names, characters, places, and incidents either are the
product of the author's imagination or are used fictitiously, and any resemblance to
actual persons, living or dead, business establishments, events, or locales is entirely
coincidental.

BOOKS ARE AVAILABLE AT QUANTITY DISCOUNTS WHEN USED TO PROMOTE PRODUCTS OR
SERVICES. FOR INFORMATION PLEASE WRITE TO PREMIUM MARKETING DIVISION, PENGUIN
PUTNAM, INC., 375 HUDSON STREET, NEW YORK, NEW YORK 10014.

# Chapter One

"Do you, William Ledbetter, take this woman for your lawful wedded wife?" the vicar asked, his expression one of both concern and expectation.

"I do," said William Ledbetter, Eighth Baron Ledbetter, his own countenance verging on impatience. It had, after all, taken the vicar half an hour to reach this point in the wedding service. Ledbetter had expected something a great deal simpler, and certainly devoid of a lengthy homily. They were, after all, in the Grand Salon of his bride's family home, surrounded by no less than twelve members of her family. He himself had only his sister present.

His sister looked every bit as bemused as the vicar.

Not so his bride's family. Her mother was positively beaming on the couple soon to be joined in holy matrimony. Her father, though more restrained, exhibited signs of relief at getting a daughter of two-and-twenty off his hands. At least two of the three sisters were in states of alt, in anticipation of their turns at a Season now Prudence was safely out of the way.

Oh, he'd done a service to the family, no doubt about it. As for Prudence herself, he was not so sure. His bride looked composed, except for a bright spot of color on each high cheekbone. She repeated her vows with no hesitation or hint of panic. She was not going to back out at the last moment.

Ledbetter did feel a moment's wariness as the vicar looked sternly round the assembled audience and requested that anyone speak out who knew why the two of them should not be joined together. Given the nature of the gathering, however, only his sister could have been expected to say anything at this moment, and Harriet had her lips firmly pressed together in a slight smile. If she had her doubts as to what kind of marriage he was making, she was keeping them to herself.

The vicar proceeded slowly and solemnly through the service, one Ledbetter assumed he must have performed dozens of times, for he was not a young man. His thatch of white hair capped a gnomish face and an aging body. The baron had been introduced to him just an hour previously, when he presented the special license he'd procured for the marriage. The vicar had perused the sheet of paper with a marked degree of skepticism, and, setting it aside, had proceeded to quiz Ledbetter.

Though the baron had been reasonably forthcoming, and had made some effort to charm the local man, Mr. Blackwood had made no similar effort. Only through the intervention of Mr. Stockworth, Prudence's father, had his agreement to perform the hasty marriage been won. Ledbetter felt under no obligation to further propitiate a man of the cloth who appeared to dispute his right to carry off a local spinster.

The groom suspected that Prudence would be sorely missed in the parish. Her major objection to the speed of the ceremony had been that she had not completed arrangements for the charity bazaar to take place the following month.

His bride now turned to face him as the vicar pronounced them man and wife. An odd sensation stole over him as he inspected the large hazel eyes. Had she any idea of whom she was marrying? Did he? Those eyes seemed so honest and straightforward—what if that was merely a trick of his imagination? He had remembered the light sprinkling of freckles across the bridge of her nose from when he had met her four years ago. And the wild, auburn hair, almost untamable with pins and combs. No beauty in the traditional sense, of course, but striking with those huge eyes and the full, provocative lips.

Her gown did not do her figure justice. There had been little time to have a suitable garment readied for the brief ceremony, so she wore a modified version of the court dress in which she had been presented to the Queen. White looked insipid against her pearly shoulders. The only thing that brought out her coloring properly was the emerald necklace Harriet had thought to bestow on her, a family heirloom which did not become his sister nearly so well as it did his bride.

"My dear," he murmured now, placing a chaste kiss on her upturned cheek. "I trust you don't share your vicar's hesitation about marrying me."

Prudence shook her head with a slight frown. "I don't know what's gotten into Mr. Blackwood," she whispered back. "He is ordinarily the most accommodating of men."

"No doubt it was the unseemly precipitation," Ledbetter suggested mildly. "But if we were to have Harriet here, we had no choice but to move matters along."

"I quite understand," Prudence said. She turned now to smile at his sister, offering her hand. "I'm delighted that you could be with us, Lady Markham. Lord Ledbetter deserved to have his only family with him on the occasion of his marriage, especially as I have so many members of my own family here."

Lady Markham pressed the hand offered to her and smiled. "I would not have missed Will's nuptials for the world. It was kind of you to accommodate my schedule, dear Lady Ledbetter."

Prudence looked momentarily startled at her new title. Ledbetter cocked his head and teased her with, "You will have to accustom yourself to your new name, my dear. No more Prudence Stockworth. I daresay your sister Elinor will delight in becoming Miss Stockworth for as long as it takes her to change it."

This plain speaking did not earn him an answering smile, for Prudence's attention had indeed already been captured by two of her sisters, who had descended upon her with gushes of excitement and waterfalls of flowery words. Ledbetter found these two a little tiresome, though the same could not be said for the youngest, Lizzie, who had a decided penchant for mischief.

He felt certain it was Lizzie who had managed to mix the soap in his shaving kit with whitewash that morning. He would have painted himself white had not his borrowed valet discovered the trick. Ledbetter could not be sure whether the prank had been done in fun or in anger. In neither case would he have informed his host, but he noticed the youngest Stockworth hanging back now, and he directed a neutral gaze upon her and beckoned with a finger.

"Don't you plan to wish us well?" he inquired when she dutifully presented herself.

A younger version of Prudence, with long auburn hair and eyes too large for her face, she looked doubtful. "I would rather Prudence weren't going away," she said.

"Lizzie!" her mother interjected. "Really, you say the oddest things, child. Lord Ledbetter will think you a graceless scamp."

"Not at all," he assured her. "She'll miss her sister. That is only to be expected." And then, no doubt owing to the headiness of the occasion, he added, "Perhaps you will come to visit us, Lizzie."

The girl blinked at him. "When?"

Having already regretted the impulse, he said offhandedly, "Sometime in the months ahead, I should think."

Lizzie met his gaze for a moment and then turned away without comment. Ledbetter felt slightly discomposed by her obvious dismissal of his poor attempt of placate her. He had, once or twice, thought he detected the same kind of bluntly dismissive attitude in Prudence, but no sooner would he try to put his finger on an instance than it would slip away, and she would seem quite unexceptionable to him again.

His bride was now receiving her parents' enthusiastic best wishes. He observed her composure with appreciation. She was astute enough to know precisely how delighted her family was with this turn of events, and how lucky they thought her, but she gave no hint that their reaction was out of the ordinary. She might have been engaged to him for three years, as she had been to the Porlonsby fellow, for all the state of nerves she exhibited.

And then it was time for him to take her in to the sumptuous breakfast her family was providing as the wedding feast. Very practical of them to arrange for an early start to the day, so that he and his bride might be on their way and travel a fair distance before halting for the night on their way to Salston. With his post chaise and four he trusted they would need but one night on the road.

Prudence placed her hand firmly on his arm and smiled up at him. "I hope you're in good appetite, my lord," she said. "Mama has been to some trouble to make this as lavish a feast as the Venetian breakfast she accompanied me to some years ago in London."

"Trust me to appreciate even the most negligible potted

viand," Ledbetter assured her. He liked the feel of her hand on his arm, liked the way she took her place beside him at the table with the ease of long association. Thank God there was no timidity here! He had been wise indeed to choose a woman of maturity rather than a green girl.

Her uncles and cousins proposed toasts. Her father and a neighbor proposed toasts. When it was Ledbetter's turn to do the honors, he lifted his glass to his bride and said, "To my wife, a treasure of beauty, intelligence, and both sense and sensibility. May I prove worthy of her love and devotion."

Harriet's brows rose at this, but Ledbetter took little notice of her skepticism. What, after all, was so difficult about being a husband? Harriet's own lord and master was hardly an example of rectitude. And yet his sister loved Markham to distraction, didn't she? There was no reason why Prudence shouldn't grow to feel an equal estimation for himself. In fact, he believed he could see it forming already. Her eyes were luminous, her lips bowed into an engaging smile. An air of sweet abandon clung to her. Would that they were alone at this very moment!

At least, Ledbetter thought that until his bride rose from the table. Then her luminescence appeared to be a product of her having drunk too much of her father's very passable champagne. Prudence stood a little unsteadily on her feet, staring owlishly at him.

"I beg your pardon!" she exclaimed, covering a hiccup with her dainty hand. "I fear I'm not accustomed to spirits at this hour of the day."

Ledbetter laughed and pressed her hand to his lips. It would do no harm for her family to see such a token of his affection. "Will you be able to change into your traveling costume?"

She nodded, but looked around hopefully and smiled with

relief when Lizzie appeared at her side. "Lizzie will come with me," she told him unnecessarily.

The baron watched her go with some misgivings. Did he really know her at all? What if she proved to be one of those women who imbibed too much alcohol on every social occasion? Or worse, who drank from morning to night. He had seen no evidence of such habits during his stay, but naturally she would be on her best behavior.

He found Harriet at his side and looked to his sister for reassurance. "I fear my bride is not accustomed to champagne," he remarked with a rueful tilt of his brows.

"All to the good," Harriet retorted as she brushed away a bit of fluff from the shoulder of his coat. "They really shouldn't let all those dogs in the house, though. That white one sheds hair like rain. You've got it on the seat of your breeches from the chair, Will."

Ledbetter gave a tsk of annoyance, but refused to be seen swatting at his rump in mixed company. "Perhaps I should put myself into that valet's hands now, anyhow," he suggested. "We have a long way to travel today if we wish to make the Crown and Scepter by nightfall."

They had left the Stockworths grouped together in the hallway, obviously awaiting Prudence's reappearance in her traveling clothes. Harriet nudged Ledbetter into a small anteroom near the front door, where applicants were left to kick their heels while waiting for the squire. "You wished to say something to me in private?" Ledbetter guessed, amusement in his voice.

"I did." Harriet walked to the window and stood there with her back to him. "You may think Miss Stockworth is more sophisticated than she is," she began.

"I beg your pardon?"

Harriet turned with a frown. "Well, she's older than the chits in London. And that's perfectly acceptable, of course.

But you may be thinking that she has the level of sophistication a married woman of her age might have."

A twinkle appeared in Ledbetter's eyes. "Are you trying to advise me on matters intimate, my adorable sister?"

Her face flushed slightly, but Harriet persisted. "I wouldn't presume to advise you on anything, Ledbetter. I'm just offering an observation. You're an accomplished flirt with women of her age, as I'm sure you would not deny. But they are women who have a level of experience that your Prudence cannot aspire to, in spite of her lengthy previous engagement."

"And why is that, my dear?"

"Don't be obtuse, Ledbetter!" Harriet gave a moue of frustration, and perhaps embarrassment. "The mild-mannered Porlonsby was in India almost the whole time they were engaged. She has no more experience of matters intimate, as you call them, than her sisters."

"Probably less," he admitted wryly, "especially that blond one. Harriet, you must think me a great deal less adept than I account myself. I'm well aware of my bride's innocence. I find it enchanting."

His sister regarded him critically. "I daresay you do. That does not mean you will know how to properly handle her innocence."

"And you wished to make me cognizant of the appropriate manner?"

There was just the slightest edge to his voice. Harriet threw up her hands in surrender. "Certainly not. I merely wished to call your attention to the possibility of your bride's . . . shyness."

"Thank you, my dear, I shall be on the lookout for it." Ledbetter picked a single white dog hair from his sleeve. "I really should change. Was there anything else?"

His sister sighed. "You could have had the money from

Markham, you know. He would have been willing to lend it to you."

Ledbetter shrugged. "I'm aware of that, Harriet. I chose to pursue my own course, as you see."

"She's a fine woman, Will," his sister admitted. "You don't deserve her, you know."

"Probably not. But I have her."

"Yes." Harriet turned again to the window. "She could be the making of you, if you let her."

"Ah, but is that likely, my dear? I'm a care-for-nothing London beau. I believe that was the expression your husband used."

"He meant it as a compliment," she retorted. "And it's quite obvious that you care for Salston."

"I do. It's my seat, and I've every intention of keeping it intact. Hence my marriage."

Harriet turned slowly to face him. "Have a care for Prudence. As your wife, she is deserving of your attention and your kindness. I trust her father insisted on an allowance befitting a baroness."

Ledbetter found himself sorely tempted to give his sister a set-down. Instead, he said with marked neutrality, "He was a great deal more astute than one would think from looking at him. Prudence will have quite a handsome allowance."

"Excellent." She opened her mouth to say something, but closed it again with a sigh.

Ledbetter approved of his sister's decision to forego any further comment. No doubt she realized how close he was to being seriously displeased with her unnecessary intervention. He could not image what possessed her to think he would act anything less than honorably with his bride, unless it was that he had married her for her inheritance from the poor deceased Porlonsby.

Which was hardly to the point, was it? Someone had to

marry her with that handsome fortune, and it might as well be he as anyone, mightn't it? What choice did a man with a title and a large draw against his estate have, after all? To have borrowed from his brother-in-law would not have suited him, and his need had been rather pressing.

Ledbetter felt a sudden desire to be on his way. He moved to stand beside his sister at the window, looking out over the gravel drive and the row of chestnut trees. "I know you mean well," he said, without looking at her. "And I'm de-lighted that you came for the ceremony, Harriet. It meant a great deal to me, having my only family here." He turned then and lifted her chin with his finger. "You worry too much. Everything will work out splendidly."

"I'm sure you're right," she agreed, if not with as much enthusiasm as he could have hoped. "Go get changed. You don't want to keep your bride waiting."

"No, indeed."

# Chapter Two

Prudence allowed her sister Lizzie to take her outside into the kitchen garden for a breath of fresh air to clear her head. "Papa wouldn't let me have any champagne," Lizzie complained. "He'd have done better to refuse to let you have any."

"Don't scold me," Prudence begged, battling hard against both dizziness and nausea. She attempted to focus on a bare vine climbing up the brick wall, but the effort made her woozy.

The March sun was weak, and little of it penetrated the walled garden. Prudence suddenly realized it might be years before she saw the Colwyck kitchen garden again. Thyme and marjoram would grow again this spring, but she wouldn't be here to pluck and dry the leaves. Something very like a sob caught in her throat.

Sympathetic now, Lizzie stroked her sister's arm and drew her down onto the bench, saying, "You'll feel better in a little while. You couldn't have had that much."

"No, but I do seem to remember Harkins refilling my glass at least twice."

Lizzie scoffed at this. "Your glass probably wasn't empty each time, Pru. He was just being attentive to the new bride." And then her face seemed to crumple. "Oh, Pru, you shouldn't have done it!"

"Nonsense!" her sister said bracingly. "He's a perfectly respectable man."

Lizzie raised her brows but made no comment.

"Well, perhaps we've heard things about him which indicate a slightly frivolous disposition, but he hasn't struck me as being the least bit objectionable these two weeks past that he's been here."

"Two weeks," her sibling moaned. "How well can you come to know a man in two weeks, Pru? He might be a wretched fellow for all we know."

"My dear child, I met him in London years ago. He was accepted everywhere. I doubt that has changed."

"No, but society is forever fawning over anyone with a title," the innocent ten-year-old proclaimed. "He would have to have done something drastic to have doors locked against him."

"You are forgetting how very respectable his sister is, and she seems to dote on him, don't you think?"

"Indeed she does. But that means nothing, Pru. There would naturally be a familial bond between them."

Prudence laughed. "Naturally? Oh, I think we've seen in our own family that familial bonds are not necessarily natural."

"Well, they are. It is just that our sisters are missing some facet of their characters. Why, Elinor could very well have waited another year to make her come-out in London. How dared she call you a millstone round her neck? She must have read such drivel in a story."

Prudence rose and smiled down at her sister. "It doesn't matter, Lizzie. She will have her chance now to go to London, as I did four years ago. I hope she may meet someone as wonderful as . . ."

Catching herself about to utter Porlonsby's name rather than that of her bridegroom, Prudence clapped a hand to her mouth and looked positively stricken. "So much has happened in the past year," she protested by way of an excuse. "I'd scarcely accustomed myself to poor Allen's death when Ledbetter showed up. I thought at first he had somehow heard of Elinor's famous beauty and come to court her by stealing a march on the London beaus."

"No, he came to win you and your money," Lizzie said bluntly.

"Yes, well, I don't begrudge it to him. Papa has arranged matters quite well, I think. I am to have an excessively large allowance. You know, I have always thought it would be delightful to dress in the first stare of fashion," she said dreamily. "Will I be expected to pay for a woman to dress me out of my allowance, do you suppose?"

Lizzie gave this matter serious thought as she guided her sister back into the house and up the stairs to the first floor. "Well, most of the staff would be Ledbetter's responsibility, but a dresser may be different. I shouldn't think one would be so very expensive, though, unless you were determined on someone with a reputation."

"Don't you think I shall need someone who has dressed some lady of fashion?" Prudence inquired.

"Hardly. My dear sister, such a woman would be stuffy beyond bearing and you would not be able to put up with her for a week." Lizzie pushed open the door to Prudence's room, only to find that Elinor and Gladys were already there.

"Where have you been?" Elinor exclaimed. "We've been waiting forever to get you into your traveling costume. You will look excessively fine in that Prussian blue," she added handsomely.

Prudence thanked her and allowed the two to strip her of her wedding gown. It had seemed eminently practical to use the court dress again, for she was certain Elinor would refuse to have it for her own presentation. The traveling costume, however, was new, an exquisitely tailored gown that flattered her feminine figure.

Elinor smoothed the fabric down over Prudence's hips, saying, "I'm sure Lord Ledbetter will have the greatest difficulty waiting until this evening to see to the disposal of these skirts. You are fortunate to have won so handsome a man, isn't she, Gladys? That should go a long way toward making her wedding night most agreeable, eh?"

Lizzie made a face behind Elinor's back. Prudence was well aware of Elinor's unfortunate lack of delicacy in discussing men and conjugal duties. Gladys was sniggering at Elinor's remarks, adding her own perception of the situation: "His experience is sure to be helpful, too, Prudence, for you may be sure he's been with any number of women. Which could not be said for poor Porlonsby, you know."

Prudence was forced to bite her lip to keep from saying something most uncharitable to her sisters. Fortunately Lizzie stepped forward to place the matching blue hat on Prudence's head with an exclamation of appreciation. "Oh, you look charming. No, no, don't tuck in that curl, Gladys. The way it escapes is positively delightful. Ledbetter will think her the most beautiful woman in Hampshire."

Though Elinor and Gladys were wont to be amused by such enthusiasm for their sister's subtle attractions, Prudence, catching sight of herself in the cheval glass, thought that indeed she was in her best looks. Her color was a little higher than usual, owing to the excitement of the occasion. Or perhaps to the champagne. Lizzie hugged her and turned her toward the door.

"You'd best be on your way," she urged.

Prudence took one last long look around her room. Her trunks were packed and gone. Such mementos as she'd collected during her engagement to Allen had been relegated to the attics or the dustbin. All save the ring he'd sent her from India. That was still tucked in a drawer of her dressing table.

Because she wanted there to be no question about who was to have his ring, she had waited until this moment to dispose of it. Taking it out of the drawer, she closed it tightly in her fist for a moment, and then handed it to Lizzie. "This is for you, my dear. You were always a great favorite of Allen's, and he would have wanted you to have it, as I no longer can. I hope you will remember him fondly, as I do."

"Oh, Prudence!" Lizzie stared at the gold band with its elegantly set ruby. "Thank you! Of course I shall treasure it, and always remember Allen with the deepest affection."

Both Elinor and Gladys were glaring at their youngest sister, but neither having had any fondness for Allen Porlonsby, nor he for them, they were helpless to protest Prudence's decision on where to bestow the treasure. Chagrin was writ large on Elinor's face, and Gladys scoffed, "Oh, Lizzie will probably lose it."

"I won't! I shall take the greatest care of it," Lizzie insisted, her eyes sparkling with a suspicion of tears.

"Of course, you will, my dear," Prudence agreed. Her own heart felt sorely tried by having to part with this last gift from her fiancé. But she could scarcely carry it with her to her new home, could she? "I believe I'm ready now to go downstairs."

Ledbetter had arrived in the Great Hall only a short time before his bride appeared. As he watched her descend the circular sweep of the staircase, he was a little surprised by the murmurs of approval greeting her appearance. Ledbetter had always considered Prudence a handsome woman; it appeared that her family had not. He heard a cousin exclaim in an easily overheard undertone, "Why, she's quite a striking thing, isn't she?"

The Prussian blue traveling costume did indeed bring out the best of her coloring, as the converted court dress had not. The hat that perched at a slight angle on her head gave her an air of mischievous insouciance. But Ledbetter could not be sure that it wasn't the young Lizzie who had made the final adjustment to the bonnet, perhaps even tweaking that excessively long feather so that it swept extravagantly behind Prudence like a misplaced halo.

He stepped forward to meet her as she came down the last few steps. "Delightful," he said, taking her hand and placing it on his arm. "Blue becomes you."

"Thank you, my lord."

"The carriage has been brought round and, if you are ready, I should like us to be on our way."

"Of course." Prudence turned to the sisters who followed her and hugged each of them in turn, holding on to Lizzie for several seconds longer than the other two. Lizzie, Ledbetter saw, had tears in her eyes. He heard her whisper, "Oh, I shall miss you, Pru. Write to me often. Promise you will!"

"I will," his bride agreed, "for with Ledbetter to frank my least significant words, I shan't hesitate to post them."

He eyed his bride sharply. Somehow it almost sounded—though of course she hadn't meant it to—as if she had married him because he could frank her letters to her sister. And there was that gleam in her eyes, the gleam he suspected meant that she was amusing herself at someone else's expense—in this case, his.

But the gleam was gone on the instant that she turned to her mother and father. With a sober demeanor she thanked them and said all that was proper on the occasion. Quickly, then, she worked her way through the other guests, only pausing when she came to his sister.

"I am so pleased that you could be here for our wedding, Lady Markham." Prudence held both of Harriet's hands in her own. "I shall try to make your brother a satisfactory wife, and I hope you will come to visit us at Salston often. There are so many things I would like to ask you; I regret we didn't have more time together."

"I regret it, too," Harriet replied, pressing the hands that held hers. "Welcome to the family, my dear. Don't hesitate to call on me at any time." She dropped her voice so the Stockworths couldn't hear, but Prudence and Ledbetter could. "The best piece of advice I received on the occasion of my marriage was to start out as I meant to go on. With someone like Will, I think you would be wise to heed it, too."

Ledbetter took exception to this counsel, but his bride merely smiled and nodded. "An excellent idea," she said. "Your brother would not wish me to pretend to a meekness which I did not possess, would he?"

Harriet's eyes sparkled with amusement. "Indeed not. My brother does not need a compliant woman for a wife. He needs someone who will meet him word for word, else he will think he can ride roughshod over you. And that would be disastrous for you both."

"My sister jests," Ledbetter hastened to interpose. He captured his bride's hand and once again placed it on his arm. With a slight frown he said to Harriet, "You will alarm my bride with such talk, dear. I'm sure I am the most reasonable of creatures, unlikely to do anything so uncivil as to ride roughshod over anyone."

Harriet's lips twitched but she merely nodded. "As you say, Will."

And then Ledbetter led Prudence out the front door and

down the stairs to the gravel drive where his carriage waited. Her family followed a discreet distance behind them, only calling out their farewells when the newlyweds were seated in the luxuriously appointed interior and the postilions had begun to move forward. Prudence waved out her window until they had passed beyond the court-yard, and then she settled back against the squabs with a sigh.

"You're tired, my dear," Ledbetter remarked. "Perhaps you could fall asleep for a space if you were to rest your head on my shoulder."

"I believe I might," Prudence agreed. "I'm afraid the champagne went to my head, and though my mind has cleared now, I feel excessively tired."

"Come, then." He leaned over to remove the delightful confection from her head, setting it carefully on the seat opposite them. Prudence still sat rather stiffly beside him and he smiled his most charming smile. The carriage swayed as they swept from the driveway onto the country road, propelling Prudence toward him. Swiftly he snared her against him with one firm arm. "There. That's just right. Tuck your head just so and you'll be asleep in no time at all."

There was no reply from his bride, though she did settle comfortably against him. He liked the weight of her on his side, and he kept his arm around her to prevent her being dislodged when the carriage bumped along the ill-paved roads. Ledbetter hadn't experienced the emotion of protec-tiveness before, and he was rather taken with the notion of having a wife to guard against the ills of climate, transport, and hunger.

Of course, he'd been protector to a number of young women in London. Sequentially, as he had no taste for the kind of bickering he'd seen between two women both in keeping by the same man. A dubious policy in any case, to his mind. Why would a man have need of more than one woman to satisfy his needs? And if a particular woman lost her appeal for you, why would you bother to keep her any longer? Any sensible man would simply offer her a handsome parting gift and move on.

All this, of course, had nothing to do with having a wife. Since Ledbetter had not had one before, he was not precisely sure whether it would be necessary to have a woman in keeping any longer, though he suspected that it would. Most of his acquaintance seemed to do so, at all events. There was a good deal of sotto voce talk of "not wishing to impose on the dear woman," with regard to a wife. Imposing on a mistress was the whole point, of course. A civilized system, he supposed, but he had a moment's pause in looking down at his sleeping bride.

It did seem a duplication of effort, to say nothing of a great waste of money, to have two women in keeping, especially if one of them was your wife. Ledbetter felt fortunate that he had no other woman in keeping at the moment, as Jenny had found a baker in Spencer Street who wished to make an honest woman of her. Well, more power to her. Ledbetter hoped she would enjoy the life of a shopkeeper as much as she had enjoyed that of a lightskirt. Certainly her husband should appreciate her lusty attitude toward life.

Given the direction of his thoughts, it was not surprising that the baron began to experience a certain physical interest in the woman whose head had gradually drifted down until it rested in his lap. A tendril of her hair curled against her flushed cheek. Her lips in sleep gave an occasional puff of breath, and the curve of her neck seemed exquisitely vulnerable. It was a pleasure to picture her in his bed, so innocent and trusting as she seemed. For though she had been engaged for a lengthy period of time, Ledbetter had it on excellent authority (from her sisters) that Prudence had scarcely become engaged before the young gentleman had journeyed off to India. No time for any real dalliance to happen between them. A few kisses, perhaps, but unlikely anything further. Ledbetter smiled and stroked the firm line of her jaw with his forefinger.

# Chapter Three

On the instant his bride was awake. She extracted herself from his lap with alacrity, exclaiming, "Oh, I beg your pardon! I had not intended to sprawl all over you, my lord. Do forgive me."

"There is nothing to forgive, ma'am," Ledbetter assured her. "You were resting so peacefully. I had no intention of disturbing you."

Prudence straightened and looked out the window as she pushed the wayward tendril back behind her ear. "We're almost to the toll road. I must have slept for half an hour."

The baron nodded. "I trust it has refreshed you."

"Yes, indeed," Prudence said brightly. She reached across to where her reticule lay on the opposite seat. "I have brought something to while away the hours, if you should not find it too dull a pastime."

Ledbetter could, perhaps, have thought of more enjoyable occupations than playing a game of chess with the clever little set his bride had brought with her. And he was not certain that her having brought it was not a bit of an insult to his conversational abilities, but, vaguely to his surprise, he found that she was by no means an unaccomplished player. Thus the afternoon passed in a mentally invigorating manner, despite the fact that he won all but one game. Ledbetter was almost surprised when they drew up at the Crown and Scepter.

As the carriage slowed, he glanced out into the darkening evening. Already torches were lit on either side of the inn door, and the host was hastening outside to welcome his noble guests. Ledbetter had sent ahead to arrange for a private parlor as well as a suite of rooms above. As soon as the stairs were let down, he climbed from the coach and reached up to hand down his companion.

Prudence was hastily donning the hat he had tossed aside earlier in their journey. She looked a little flustered, as though she had been caught *en déshabille*. Well, his sister would not have stepped out of a carriage without her hat, either, but he had trained Harriet to prepare ahead for these contingencies. He was not a patient man, and he was accustomed to others accommodating him so that he was not forced to cool his heels. But it was his wedding day, and his bride was unaccustomed to his ways, so he stood with his hand outstretched to her for quite a full minute until she was ready to descend.

The landlord, a short, round-faced man, wiped his hands on the clean apron around his middle and begged them to enter his hostelry. "Your horses will be given the greatest care, my lord," he assured them as he led the way. "I believe the Crown and Scepter has a well-deserved reputation for our services. This is Mrs. Granger," he said, introducing an amiable-looking woman of middle age. "She will see to my lady's comfort."

Mrs. Granger dropped a curtsy to Prudence and said, "You'll be wanting to have a bit of a tidy up before you dine, my lady. Let me show you to your room."

Prudence smiled gratefully at her. "Yes, that is exactly what I need, Mrs. Granger. Thank you." She turned to the landlord and said, "Will you see that the small trunk is sent up, sir? That's all I will require."

And a great deal less than his sister would have, Ledbetter thought ruefully as he watched Prudence gather her skirts and ascend the staircase behind the energetic Mrs. Granger. He noticed, as he had not on previous occasions, that his new wife had a very fine set of ankles.

"Perhaps your lordship would care for a glass of brandy to wash the dust of the road away," the landlord suggested, indicating the open door to the taproom, from which emerged the sounds of conviviality.

"I believe I would," he agreed, and made his way through the narrow door into the low-ceilinged room.

A smoking fire had filled the space with a light haze. Ledbetter settled himself at a table near the window and the landlord brought him a glass of brandy. It was a relief to be out of the jolting carriage and seated so solidly on the wooden chair, and Ledbetter relaxed back against the spindle back with a sigh. He lifted the amber liquid and took a healthy sip, allowing the fiery drink to refresh and invigorate him.

At the tables around him were men in groups, mostly drinking ale. Some travelers, some local people, all fortifying themselves against the cool evening. One old fellow was in the midst of a long story to which the others seemed to be paying considerable attention. Ledbetter sipped at his brandy and soon found himself caught up in the unending tale of a young man who had run away to sea at an early age, only to find himself left behind in Africa after a bout of near-fatal illness. His adventures in making his way home to England had every man in the taproom shaking his head, or laughing, as the tale progressed.

Ledbetter only realized when the landlord came to inform him of her ladyship awaiting him in his private parlor that he had consumed two glasses of brandy, and allowed a significant amount of time to pass. Hell, he hadn't even gone abovestairs to tidy himself! He polished off the last of the brandy in his glass and rose hastily. It wouldn't do to keep Prudence waiting on their wedding day—though he was sorely tempted to hear the outcome of the story.

Across the passage he found his bride seated on a velvet sofa, her hands employed with knitting needles. Knitting needles! Good Lord, what had possessed her to bring knitting on their wedding journey? Ledbetter settled himself beside her on the sofa and said, "I hope I haven't kept you waiting."

When Prudence met his gaze, he was surprised to see what he took for a flash of impatience in her eyes. But all she replied was, "Not at all, my lord. We did not set any time for meeting here. I had merely assumed that I would take longer in my preparations than you would."

It seemed to him that she was surveying him then, judging that he had not cleaned himself up at all after their journey. But Ledbetter had no inclination to explain himself. Instead he nodded to her knitting and asked, "What is it that you're working on?"

"Oh, just a shawl that I had started for the charity bazaar before we made the decision to marry. I shan't finish it in time to send, of course, but I'm not one for idle hands. I had the work in my trunk, and I asked Mrs. Granger to bring it to me when I found that I would have a little time to work on it."

Ledbetter considered this a criticism of him for not being in the private parlor when she arrived there. Certainly he had intended to precede her there, and possibly to have already ordered their meal so that they could dine without delay.

But it was early yet, if not by country hours, then by those which governed in London. Granted, they had had nothing to eat since the large wedding breakfast. He supposed his bride was hungry and had come down expecting to be fed. "Shall I order our meal now?" he asked.

"That would be kind of you," she said, not lifting her gaze from the green wool passing so quickly through her fingers. "I did ask Mrs. Granger if she would bring me a hot cup of tea and a biscuit or two while I waited. I'm afraid we eat rather early at home."

Which of course he knew perfectly well, having been there for most of the last two weeks. Ledbetter had the distinct impression that they were not starting off on the right foot here. He hated being put at a disadvantage. But he was not accustomed to considering anyone else's welfare and schedule but his own. It would take time for him to adjust to this new start, as even his bride must know. He was considering whether to apologize to her when Mrs. Granger arrived with a tea tray.

Prudence smiled graciously as the landlady arranged the tray on a small table beside the sofa. Mrs. Granger had brought a plate full of dainty cakes for Prudence's enjoyment and Ledbetter thought that if she ate all of them, she would have no appetite at all for her meal. But that was what came of letting the poor woman starve, he supposed.

Mrs. Granger suggested that they might like salmon dressed with cucumbers and a roast fowl, with side dishes of stewed mutton kidneys and rissoles. Ledbetter approved the menu, before remembering to ask his bride if it was agreeable to her.

"Quite agreeable," she said as she poured herself a cup of tea. "Shall I have Mrs. Granger bring a cup for you, Ledbetter?"

"No, thank you. I'll wait for ale with my meal."

Mrs. Granger curtsied and hurried off to see to the various dishes, leaving the newlyweds to a heavy silence. Ledbetter eventually asked, "Are the rooms to your liking, Prudence?"

"Perfectly satisfactory. It's a well-run inn, from all I can see. I have not myself traveled much, but I understand that one can often judge the merit of the inn by the quality of the linen. And if that is true, the Crown and Scepter has much to recommend it, for I believe both the sheets and the towels are practically new. Nothing faded or mended about either of them. And well aired, too, from my cursory inspection."

Ledbetter hadn't been expecting a detailed report, especially from someone who probably hadn't stayed at an inn above half a dozen times in her life. But he realized that Prudence was making an effort to keep their conversation moving forward, so he said, "Good, good."

Prudence took a sip of her tea and settled back against the sofa. With a small gesture she indicated the plate of cakes. "Would you like one, Ledbetter? Or would it spoil your appetite for the salmon?"

He had that feeling again that she was mocking him, and yet he could see not so much as a gleam in her eyes. "I think not, thank you. But please, help yourself if you are inclined."

"Oh, I will," she agreed, reaching a languid hand toward the plate and hesitating above first one cake and then another. "It is so hard to decide, when they all look so tempting. But I think . . . yes, the one with the nonpareils on it. I'm partial to nonpareils; are you?"

Ledbetter hadn't the slightest notion what nonpareils were, but following her hand as it reached for one of the cakes, he concluded that they were bits of colored sugar lavished on the item which she daintily picked up and transported to her waiting lips. She took a delicate bite and returned the rest of the cake to its spot on the plate. Ledbetter watched her chew the morsel with every evidence of enjoyment.

"Ah, just like the ones Cook used to make," she said with

a sigh. "I wonder if your cook will have as fine a repertoire as ours has."

Ledbetter felt his back stiffen. "I'm sure my chef is a very talented fellow. Makes every English dish that you care to mention, as well as a splendid assortment of French and Spanish dishes. I'm sure you will find his work more than satisfactory."

"Oh, yes, of course." Prudence reached toward the plate again, but did not pick up the sprinkled confection. This time she lifted a yellow square that looked very much like it might be lemon-flavored. "We called these buttercups," she said, before conveying it to her mouth for a bite. "Mmm. Very tasty. I wonder if Mrs. Granger makes them herself. I understand the landlady often does at an inn such as this."

He was sure she was poking fun at him, but he could not for the life of him decide just how. Besides, he had developed a real hunger for the most recent cake, which he felt quite certain no one had ever called a buttercup. He and everyone else in the civilized world called them lemon squares. And was she going to take a bite out of each cake, without bothering to finish it? Apparently she was. She replaced the lemon square on the plate and her hand hovered above yet another cake—this one with a crinkled surface. Ledbetter was certain it contained treacle, and was one of his very favorite pastries.

"Now these," she said, after sinking her teeth into the cake, "have been made with just the right strength of treacle. There are those," she said darkly, "who refuse to use the strongest treacle, and their biscuits and cakes are, in my humble opinion, a failure for that very reason."

"I can see that you will be very exacting about our menus," Ledbetter offered, wishing very much that he had agreed to helping himself to one of the cakes. It was too late now, as she'd managed to nibble on three of the four, and was apparently about to sample the last as well.

"Now you are not to worry about that. I shan't interfere in any substantial way with your kitchens. I may just have a word with your housekeeper about how matters are conducted at Salston, so that I will know how to go on there. Your sister gave me to understand that the housekeeper—a Mrs. Collins, I believe—is quite a straightforward woman, and one who is easy to deal with. Since your sister's marriage, I daresay you have had more contact with Mrs. Collins."

Ledbetter, who had pretty much allowed Mrs. Collins to do as she pleased on those occasions when he was at Salston, murmured his concurrence. It seemed to him that on his rare visits there, Mrs. Collins had merely brought menus for his approval, and perhaps queried him as to whether he had any special requests. The housekeeper had been at Salston since he was young, and she knew his preferences as well as his sister did. "Mrs. Collins is very accommodating," he assured her. "I'm sure she will welcome someone to give her direction and manage the household. I confess that I am not myself much interested in linens and silver."

"No, of course not," his bride agreed. She paused to taste the fourth cake, cocked her head, and frowned just slightly. "Now I wonder what gives it that slightly bitter taste? Not that it is unpleasant, mind you, but there is just a bit of an edge to it. Perhaps one of the stronger nuts, or a liqueur. Hmm. Well, I shall ask Mrs. Granger later. It could well be some Indian spice—cardamom or the like. Though I have been sent a number to experiment with, I fear I did not know precisely how to use them, and they have mostly languished on the shelf."

Just in case he had forgotten her India-dwelling former fiancé, Ledbetter thought she had managed to remind him.

Really, if she wasn't putting him on, she had suddenly taken to quite inconsequential chatter in a manner which was most unlike her. Or at least what little he knew of her. Hell, if their meal didn't come soon, he might be forced to descend to that level as well.

There was a scraping at the door of the private parlor, and the landlord entered with a tray of covered dishes. A minion followed behind him, who hastened to spread a cloth on the dining table at the far end of the room near the fireplace. Places were laid for the two of them, and the covers removed so that tempting smells drifted over to entice Ledbetter to his dinner. When the landlord had begged them to inform him of anything they lacked, Ledbetter led his bride to the table and pulled out her chair with great ceremony. "My lady," he murmured.

"My lord," she replied, but with that faint twist to her lips that seemed to indicate she found the title just slightly ridiculous.

Disgruntled, Ledbetter took his seat and raised his glass of ale. "To a long and prosperous life together."

Her smile became genuine and she raised her glass as well. "Yes, indeed. To a long and prosperous life . . . together."

# Chapter Four

Prudence had made every effort to entertain her bride-groom during their meal. She had, in fact, abandoned the whimsy that had overcome her when she was left stranded in the private parlor, to converse sensibly and intelligently with Ledbetter. This had, in turn, obviously pleased and reassured him. So much so that when an old case clock in the inn entry struck the hour of ten, Ledbetter shook his head with surprise.

"I had no idea it was so late, my dear. But there is no need for us to make an early start in the morning. We'll make Salston by late afternoon if we leave here before eleven."

His expression, one of pointed anticipation, made the hairs at Prudence's nape stand on end. Her wedding night. A very different one than she had thought to have for the last many years. Ledbetter was not Allen, whom she could have trusted to show her every consideration.

Her sisters were forever hinting at the pleasures of the flesh, at the benefits of having a man like a stallion who would enter a woman with that serviceable implement of his and . . . and what? Impregnate her, surely, as the stallions on the estate did with the mares. But humans were scarcely built on the same model, with all that nerve-shattering drumming of hooves and equine screaming.

Aware that Ledbetter was regarding her curiously, Prudence hastily rose. "I'll go up and prepare for the night, if you will excuse me."

He rose and bowed slightly to her. Then he surprised her by lifting her hand to his lips and kissing her nerveless fingers. "I'll be along shortly," he promised.

Her smile flickered briefly and disappeared. As she made her way abovestairs, Prudence kept repeating to herself, "This, too, shall pass," as though she were about to have a tooth drawn. But she felt a tightness in the pit of her stomach which would not leave her.

Mrs. Granger had spread her nightgown on the bed and Prudence thought it looked like a shroud. The abigail who had waited on Prudence and her sisters would have liked to come with Lady Ledbetter to her new home, but Prudence had objected to having the giddy young thing as her dresser. "I will choose someone from the neighborhood," she had insisted. But right now she would have welcomed even Sissy there with her to calm her nerves and assist her out of the thousand buttons of her traveling costume. Her own fingers trembled slightly as she worked her way down the front of the gown, and it was not from any chill, as there was a good fire burning in the grate.

Prudence stepped out of her gown and hung it in the armoire, allowing her hand to linger on the lovely fabric. She could have any gown she chose, now. They could all be ordered with no thought to somberness, as her self-imposed period of mourning for Allen was over. And they could be rich, flattering colors instead of the pastels which dulled her looks to obscurity, too.

Prudence turned to the dressing table across from the bed and peered at herself in the mirror. The high color that had carried her through the better part of the day had faded now. Her face looked pale and tight. She dropped onto the bench in front of the glass and began to release her auburn hair from the pins that held it in place. The thick tresses spilled down beyond her shoulders. She picked up the hairbrush Mrs. Granger had laid out and began to pull it through her hair with long, calming strokes. *This, too, shall pass.*

Then she heard movement in the room next door and her reflection in the mirror aped her dismay. He was there already, probably stripping off his neckcloth at this very moment. Prudence swallowed hard and rose, allowing the hairbrush to drop to the floor without noticing. In a panic to be clothed in her nightgown before he came to her, she tugged off her shift and underclothing, catching a glimpse of herself naked in the glass. With a low moan, she grabbed the nightgown and pulled it on, allowing the filmy material to flow easily down over her vulnerable body.

Torn as to whether or not to leave the candle burning, she bit her lip and glanced toward the connecting door. He would bring his own candle, wouldn't he? But if there was no light in her room, she would seem unwelcoming, wouldn't she? Well, she didn't welcome him, her baser self insisted. Still, she had married him. He had every right to expect her to be ready for him to . . . do whatever it was he wished to do to her.

*This, too, shall pass.*

Prudence climbed into bed after moving the candle as far away as possible, so that its faint gleam scarcely reached her. Probably he would snuff it in any case, as well as his own, to leave them in the dark. Oh, God. She couldn't do this. Not now, not tonight. It had been a long and difficult day. But if not tonight, she would just be prolonging the alarming moment. She pulled the covers up to her chin, holding them there with whitened knuckles.

Ledbetter tied the sash of his dressing gown around his waist. Then he ran his fingers through his coal black hair and frowned at his reflection in the mirror. She would be expecting him to look elegant, but how could one in a dressing gown, for God's sake? Especially one of *his* dressing gowns, chosen exclusively for their warmth in the drafty rooms at Salston. Frankly, Ledbetter was not certain any man could look elegant and sophisticated unless he was wearing a neckcloth, and you surely could not wear one with a dressing gown.

And would she be expecting him to be wearing something *under* his dressing gown? His cotton drawers, perhaps. Ledbetter was not accustomed to wearing anything at all to bed. He preferred it that way, even when the sheets were cold. Which surely would not be the case tonight, since his bride would have had the sense to use the warming pan on both her side of the bed and his. Wouldn't she?

But then, what if she had done that some time ago, and the bed was cold again?

Ledbetter made a snort of disgust. Oh, the hell with all that. He picked up his candle and walked purposefully toward the door which led into the second room of the suite. But there he hesitated, wondering if he should knock. What if she was a very slow undresser and she was still dithering about in the middle of the room, half clothed?

Well, too bad, he decided, though he did just give a tap to the door before he opened it and walked through. There was a candle burning on the chest of drawers, but scarcely enough light to reach the four-poster bed. He couldn't see her at all in the shadows, though he felt certain she must be in the bed. He snuffed her candle, kept his in hand and advanced toward the bed.

Her face looked even paler against the white linens than it had looked before she came abovestairs. The sprinkling of freckles seemed to stand out on the bridge of her nose.

Her eyes were closed, but Ledbetter felt sure she wasn't asleep.

"Prudence?"

Her eyes fluttered open and she regarded him silently.

"Do you mind if I join you in bed?" he asked.

"Yes," she said, though there was a total lack of expression on her face.

"You do mind if I join you?" he asked, surprised.

Her mouth opened and closed a few times, before she managed to say, "I'm afraid I . . . don't feel very well."

"Ah," he said. Now what? Ledbetter supposed he must graciously leave her if she didn't feel well. "Poor dear. It's been a trying day for you. Can I send for anything? Mrs. Granger probably has a soothing draught if you would like it. Is it your stomach?"

"No. Yes. Everything."

Hmm. "I see." Though of course he didn't. "Well, my dear, if there's nothing I can get for you, I will say good night."

"No, no, nothing. I feel certain I'll be perfectly all right in the morning."

"Yes, of course. A good night's sleep will set you up just right, I daresay." Ledbetter could not be positive, but in the wavering light of the candle his bride already looked better. A little color had seeped back into her cheeks even as they spoke. Very odd. "I shan't keep you, then. Sleep well."

"Thank you, Ledbetter. I do hope I shall."

He had already turned away when he felt a strong compulsion to kiss her. She was, after all, his bride. This was, for better or worse, his wedding day. He turned back and was considerably startled to see a single tear sliding down her cheek. "My dear, you are in some pain," he protested, crouching down beside the bed. "Please tell me what I can do."

"No, no, it is just the upset," she whispered, not meeting his gaze. "Really, it is nothing, Ledbetter. You needn't concern yourself."

"My dear girl, who should be more concerned than your husband? If there is nothing I can get for you, perhaps I should stay until you sleep."

"Please don't," she pleaded. "Truly, I will be perfectly fine if only I am left alone to recover myself."

Slightly offended, Ledbetter rose once more to his feet. "As you wish, of course. But please don't hesitate to call me should you need me during the night. I will leave the connecting door open so that I may hear you."

Her sigh looked almost like a shudder, but she nodded and thanked him. Ledbetter decided he would not, after all, kiss her. What was the point? Better not to tease those expectant loins of his any further than they had already been tempted by the knowledge of this being his wedding night. Tomorrow was soon enough to satisfy the craving that roiled in him. If he were a patient man, it would hardly have bothered him at all.

In his own room he disposed of his dressing gown and climbed between the icy sheets. He left his candle to burn itself down in a misguided effort to provide his new wife with a reassuring beacon in the dark. Sometime during the night he must have heard the faint click as the door between the two rooms was closed, but it did not disturb his sleep.

Prudence slept little, mainly because she was distressed with herself for her foolishness. Had she not agreed to marry the baron? Did she not know full well what that meant? Of course she did, and she was being the greatest beast in nature to pretend to an illness that she did not feel. At least, what she felt was not a physical illness.

Her distress, and fear, and grief had all seemed to tangle together when she looked up to see Ledbetter standing there. Not until she said it did she have any realization that she was going to send him away. And then to have him see her shed a tear! Really, she was beyond hope.

In the middle of the night she had risen to close that offending door, and subsequently wander about her room feeling wretched. The night outside was dark, with not even a quarter moon to light the stable yard over which her room looked. She could hear the occasional sounds of an owl or some creature of the wild, but within the inn there was total silence. The taproom must have closed long since, and even the Grangers gone to their beds.

Ledbetter's room had been dark when she gently pushed the door closed. Doubtless he was sleeping soundly, after wondering briefly at his bride's odd behavior. Tonight she would do better, Prudence promised herself as the first stray glimmers of dawn lit the sky. Tonight they would be at Salston, where she would have to prove herself a good and proper wife. Prudence groaned and climbed back into bed, where sleep finally overtook her.

When she awakened again, she felt disoriented. The bed was not familiar to her, nor the room. And the daylight seemed to indicate that the day was much advanced beyond the early hour at which she normally arose. Frowning, she sat up in bed, only to be overwhelmed by the realization of where she was—and who she was. The newest Lady Ledbetter.

Her gaze flew to the connecting door between his room and hers. It remained tightly closed, and she could not hear sounds issuing from the next room. Surely Ledbetter would be up by now. And if he were up, would he not have checked on her? Prudence could picture him tapping softly and entering her room when she was sound asleep. She could see him cross the rugged carpet to look down on her and find that she looked perfectly healthy, as she had the previous day. Oh, he would not be fooled. He would know she was faking her illness, and he would be furious with her.

A knock on her door startled her, and she grabbed at the bedclothes, pulling them up around her. But then she realized it was the door to the corridor from which the sound had issued, and she forced herself to call, "Enter."

Mrs. Granger peeked around the door, her face full of concern. But when she saw Prudence sitting up, she smiled broadly. "Just as I told his lordship. A night's sleep has done you a world of good, my lady. I trust you are feeling better."

"Much better," Prudence acknowledged. "Is . . . is Ledbetter next door?"

"Oh, no. He's made a hearty breakfast and gone out to see to the horses. Seems one of them threw a shoe yesterday, which no one noticed until this morning. Shall I send for him?"

"Oh, no! I shall be up directly. He must be fretting to be on the road."

"Well, the blacksmith is here and seeing to the shoeing, so there's no need to rush, my lady. Shall I bring you a cup of tea and some breakfast in your room?"

"Thank you. And if there is a girl who could help me to dress before my meal arrives, I would be grateful."

Mrs. Granger assured her that she would send Tessie right along, and almost before Prudence had her feet on the floor there was a scraping at the door. Half afraid that it would be Ledbetter, Prudence called for her visitor to enter. The girl who slipped into the room appeared no more than six-and-ten, but her resemblance to Mrs. Granger seemed to mark her as one of the family. She was quick and competent. Well before her mother arrived with Prudence's breakfast she had their guest disposed into the gown she had packed for the second day of her journey. While Prudence ate, Tessie packed away everything that had been laid out for her the night before.

"Shall I have the trunk taken down, my lady?" she asked as Prudence took the last sip of her tea.

"Thank you, yes. Has Lord Ledbetter's trunk gone down?"

"Oh, yes, but they've been seeing to the shoeing, so there was no way you could have left sooner." The girl grinned at her, adding, "Not that his lordship would be hinting otherwise, of course. But Lord Ledbetter has stayed here before, and he's always that imp . . . ready to be away, you see."

"Yes, I do see." Prudence studied the young woman thoughtfully. "Are you the Grangers' daughter, Tessie?"

"I am that. There are four of us, ma'am, all girls."

"Just like my own family. And are you the oldest, too?"

Tessie shook her head. "The third. Only Jessie is younger, and she's seven-and-ten."

Prudence considered. "So you're older than you look."

"Almost twenty, my lady." Tessie wrinkled her nose. "We're all small, so folks think we're children. Jane and Margaret are married with little ones of their own. But folks still take them for schoolgirls."

"Very annoying," Prudence said. Her mind was strongly seized with the idea of making this young woman her dresser. Something about her . . . Well, her lack of awe at Ledbetter, for one thing. Prudence did not want an abigail who fawned over her or her husband. And Tessie would have experience of waiting on ladies from having worked at the inn.

"Will there be anything else, my lady?" Tessie asked.

Prudence frowned. "No, yes. Tessie, would you be at all interested in coming to Salston? I'm in need of an abigail or a dresser. Perhaps I should see what awaits me there, but I think you would serve admirably as my personal servant."

She noted the girl's surprise, and hedged. "Well, I daresay your parents would be hard-pressed to lose you. And there may be a young man in the neighborhood here whom you should not like to leave. Or . . ."

"Oh, I would like nothing better than to work at Salston!" the young woman declared. "May I? His lordship wouldn't object?"

It had not occurred to Prudence that her husband might object. Why should he? The choice of a personal servant was surely entirely hers to make. But she hesitated, just long enough to make Tessie take a step backwards and say, "It's of no consequence, truly. I see that you were just considering the possibility and . . ."

"Tessie, is there some reason you feel Lord Ledbetter would object to your working at Salston?" Such as, that you or one of your sisters has been in his keeping, or something on that order? Prudence hated this direction of her mind, but the question had occurred to her and she did not wish to commit a truly egregious *faux pas*.

"Why, no, ma'am. But Salston is such a large, elegant establishment, and most of the servants come from the immediate neighborhood. Perhaps his lordship wouldn't like the daughter of an innkeeper to serve there."

Prudence was torn. She did not wish to displease her husband, and she had no knowledge of his hiring policies. But it seemed to her that she would do best—as his sister had suggested—to start out as she meant to go on, at least in this matter of whom she would surround herself with. Prudence did not mean to consult her husband on these domestic decisions, unless it was clear that Salston heritage was somehow involved. And she very much doubted that such a thing could apply to her choice of a dresser.

"Why don't you send your mother to me, Tessie?" Prudence suggested. "The two of us can talk the matter over and come to a decision, if that will be satisfactory to you."

"Yes, ma'am." Tessie dropped her a curtsy and hurried from the room.

# Chapter Five

"I don't understand," Ledbetter said. He had found his wife in the private parlor, looking a little peaked but not otherwise unwell. His brows drew together in a frown as he drew his gloves impatiently through his hands. "You've hired the serving girl from the Crown and Scepter for your abigail?"

His bride regarded him with a steady gaze. "Yes, that's correct. She's the Grangers' daughter, she's almost twenty and her mother has agreed that she may come."

"She can't possibly have any experience as an abigail. Mrs. Collins can help you find a local girl who will serve you better."

"But I have already hired Tessie," Prudence said with exaggerated patience. "Are you telling me that I may not hire whomever I wish?"

"Of course not." Ledbetter felt he was being put in an untenable position. He tried reasoning with his impulsive bride. "But you know, my dear, that in coming to a new household you would make a very favorable impression on Mrs. Collins if you were to trust her judgment on who would best serve you at Salston. She is a very knowledgeable woman, who has guided the household for more years than I can remember. I had thought you intended to rely on her when you decided not to bring your abigail from home."

"Perhaps I did, but I was very taken with Tessie Granger.

It will be a step up in the world for her, and I feel she will appreciate it and make the most of it." Her brows rose questioningly. "Is there some particular reason you don't wish me to have Tessie Granger at Salston?"

He found her question irritating. Surely he didn't *have* to have a reason for not wanting the girl to be his wife's abigail. Hell, the child looked like she should still be in short skirts—if it was the one he thought it was. Ledbetter felt certain the Grangers had more than one daughter. He drummed his gloves against his thigh in an excess of frustration. "How would she get to Salston? You don't intend for her to share the carriage with us, do you?"

Astonished, his wife exclaimed, "Of course not! Her father will drive her over at the end of the week." She rose and stood facing him, a slightly more conciliating expression on her pale face. "May I consider it finished then, Ledbetter? Are you agreeable to her coming?"

"If you are determined upon it," he said grudgingly.

"Thank you."

So this was what marriage was like, he thought. Already his bride had kept him from her bed and hired an inn's serving girl to wait on her at Salston, home of the Barons Ledbetter for three generations. What would she do next?

"If you are quite finished here," he said, his manner a little stiff, "perhaps we could be on our way."

Prudence spent most of the day trying to placate her bridegroom. In the carriage she disposed herself carefully so as not to fall asleep and end up in his lap again. With great attention she listened to his answers to her many questions about Salston: when was it built, in which generations had it been added to, what was the closest village, did Ledbetter have the gift of the parish living, was there a large staff, and did most of them come from the area, etc., etc.

At first Ledbetter answered rather formally, but he was obviously proud of his heritage and soon Prudence had him talking with enthusiasm about the estate and its farms and the locale. There were questions she asked he did not know the answers to, which a little shocked her, but she did not dwell on them. Perhaps, after all, her father would not know whether there was a school for the farm children, or the ages of the gatekeeper's children.

Her mental picture of Salston grew with each hour they progressed toward it. Late in the afternoon Ledbetter smiled and said, "And here, at last, we've arrived. Down the avenue of oaks you can see the towers. And when we come around this bend . . . There. That is your new home, my dear Prudence. I hope you will be happy here."

"I'm sure I shall."

Prudence had grown up in a fine old manor house, but Salston appeared more on the order of a castle. She could see the whole facade now, from the corner tower on the east to that on the west. The central, stepped-back portion was topped with an immense clock tower above a heavily decorated porch. There were pierced balconies and lovely strap work. The stone looked a warm gold and the myriad windows flashed in the waning sunlight.

"It's beautiful," Prudence whispered, somewhat overcome by its magnificence. "And so graceful. Every room must be filled with light from all those windows."

The carriage drew to a halt in front of the beautiful stone porch. The steps were let down, and the door thrown open on the instant. Ledbetter jumped down and turned to hand her out. Already a footman was hurrying down the shallow stairs to come to their assistance. The enormous doors into the main hall were thrown open and Prudence could see that the entry was lined with servants to welcome Ledbetter and his bride to Salston.

This time Prudence had arranged her hat and pelisse before arrival. She accepted Ledbetter's hand and stepped eagerly down to the ground. She knew that a great deal was expected of her in the next few minutes, and she felt perfectly capable of sustaining her role. Ledbetter put her hand on his arm and regarded her with approval. "Let me introduce you to the staff," he said as he led her up the shallow steps and into the Great Hall.

Prudence was first made known to the butler, Jenkins, and then to the housekeeper, Mrs. Collins, who in turn named each of the others—footmen and maids—lined up for her inspection. Prudence repeated each name and offered a warm smile. There were not as many employees as she had feared, but that was probably because Ledbetter had not been much in residence. Prudence then thanked them all for their welcome and said how much she looked forward to living at Salston.

Ledbetter indicated his appreciation of her gracious words with a satisfied nod. "I think, Mrs. Collins, that we should show my bride her suite of rooms before we undertake any tour of Salston. There is plenty of time for her to get acquainted with the state rooms. Right now she must wish to refresh herself before we dine."

A grand staircase rose from the opposite side of the hall, and Prudence followed Mrs. Collins and her husband up to the first floor. They made a turn to the right, heading for the East Wing. Ledbetter explained that she would have his mother's suite, as he had taken over his father's some years before. "You'll want to redecorate it, no doubt," he said, "for it's rather old-fashioned. But I'm much inclined to keep the integrity of the rooms themselves as they are an original part of the building. The furnishings and hangings, carpets and draperies—all those can be replaced."

"Perhaps in time," she said. "First I need to learn my way around and gain a sense of Salston."

Mrs. Collins paused before a heavy oak door on the left of the hall. "This will be your suite, my lady. Lord Ledbetter's suite is directly across the hall."

Prudence experienced a small spasm of nerves at this announcement, but she smiled bravely as the housekeeper pushed open the door. "Oh, how delightful."

The room was enormous, and on three surfaces there were unseasonable flowers which must have come from the estate succession houses. Candles were already lit in the sconces and the canopied bed was draped with wine velvet hangings. The furniture was of a heavy dark wood, and the carpet a pattern of wine and rose shades. Prudence walked the length of the room to the windows and drew aside the cream-colored curtains. She could just see a vast rolling lawn in the last of the daylight.

"If I might show your ladyship the rest of the suite," Mrs. Collins suggested.

"Of course." Prudence followed her through two smaller, though no less elegant, chambers, one serving as a dressing room and the other as a private sitting room. Prudence made appropriate remarks on how lovely they were, aware that Ledbetter was watching her reactions with interest. And indeed they were sumptuous rooms, far and away more elegant than anything she had experienced at home.

Ledbetter stepped forward then and said, "Thank you, Mrs. Collins. I'll show my wife the rest of the East Wing if you will arrange for us to dine in an hour."

"Certainly, my lord." Mrs. Collins looked a little surprised at this dismissal, but she turned to leave, adding only that hot water would be brought to my lady's room directly. Prudence watched her go with some alarm. She was not best pleased to be left alone with Ledbetter.

He tucked her hand in his arm and led her back into the corridor. "Mrs. Collins won't breach the inner sanctum of my suite, so I thought I'd best show it to you myself," he said. He reached down to open the door with his free hand, maintaining his link with her arm. There were candles lit in the sconces in his room as well, and the man who had been introduced as his valet, a small Frenchman called Balliot, was already unpacking Ledbetter's trunk.

"If you will excuse us, Balliot," he drawled, "I'll ring for you when I need you."

"Very good, my lord," the man said without glancing in Prudence's direction. He bowed slightly before disappearing through the far door.

"One of the reasons I objected to your hiring the Granger girl," Ledbetter remarked, "was because of Balliot."

Prudence raised her brows questioningly, and Ledbetter shrugged. "They'll be on equal footing in the household hierarchy, being our personal servants. And yet your Tessie doesn't know the first thing about serving as an abigail, let alone a dresser. Balliot will be offended, I can promise."

"I'm sorry for it, but I don't believe that objection holds any more sway with me than Tessie's inexperience, Ledbetter. I would be most surprised if she weren't perfectly capable of doing an excellent job in any capacity she filled."

"Perhaps." Though he looked unconvinced, Ledbetter was apparently willing to allow the subject to drop for the present. He motioned around him with a careless hand. "My bedroom, as you see. I haven't found any reason to change it much since I moved in here, but then I haven't spent much time at Salston." He looked about himself as though he were seeing if for the first time and a slight frown formed on his brow. "Everything is serviceable, but perhaps the trappings are a bit worn. It's probably been more than thirty years since a major renovation was undertaken."

"It's a strikingly handsome room," Prudence allowed. A very masculine room, with little ornamentation, and a richness to the hangings and carpeting that spoke of lack of concern for expense. The ceilings were especially high, with fine moldings and two ancient beams that brought to mind an earlier age.

Ledbetter strolled to the windows and drew back the curtains, but darkness had set in firmly now and little could be seen. "My view is toward the carriage drive and the stables off to the east. In the distance you can see the village church spire." He allowed the draperies to fall and turned his gaze on her.

"My mother died a little over a year ago," he said. "She died in her bed, as I suppose we all would wish to do. And yet . . ." He paused, looking for the right words. "In a house this age, generations have come and gone, they've lived and died in most rooms of the house, I daresay. I don't mean to be sentimental, or maudlin, and I most certainly want you to have her suite of rooms."

"But . . ."

"But I should prefer our . . . marital relations to occur here," he said firmly, nodding to the substantial bed. "I realize that is unusual, and I want you to understand the reason. In time, I image I will grow accustomed to your being in the room which was my mother's, and to our . . . joining in the bed where she died, but for the present, I hope you will accommodate my whimsy."

Prudence swallowed hard and forced herself to nod.

"Excellent." Ledbetter waved a hand toward the door at the far end of the room. "My suite is much like yours, actually, with a dressing room and a sitting room beyond. Unless you are inclined to see them now, I will allow you to return to your own. You'll be wishing to change before we dine."

There was very little Prudence wanted more than to es-

cape him. "Yes, indeed," she murmured, backing away from
him.

During dinner, and while she waited for Ledbetter to join
her in the blue drawing room, and even after he sat down beside her on the sofa, Prudence couldn't help but wonder how
this was supposed to work, this "marital relations" endeavor.
Was she expected to change into her nightdress and scurry
across the hall to his room? And it didn't make her any too
happy to think of his mother having died in that bed, either,
poor woman.

Ledbetter observed her closely when he had taken his seat
on the sofa only a few feet from her. "You look well. I trust
you are feeling none of the discomfort you suffered from
last night."

"I am in perfect health," she assured him. "It was a passing indisposition."

"I'm pleased to hear it." He studied the contents of his
brandy glass for a moment before lifting his gaze once more
to her face. "I daresay you may have suffered from a bout of
nerves last night, my dear Prudence. That would not have
been at all surprising. This decision of ours to marry has
been rather abrupt. You haven't had much time to accustom
yourself to the idea."

Since he seemed to be awaiting her reply, Prudence said,
"No, I haven't. But then neither have you."

Ledbetter laughed. "It's hardly the same thing for me."
He reached across and clasped her hands in his. Her fingers
were both icy and slightly trembling; he could not fail to notice either. His brows rose but he did no more than purse his
lips. "Do you think you could be frank with me about this,
Prudence?"

"F-F-Frank?"

Keeping her fingers tightly clasped in his own, he offered

a long, frustrated sigh. "I suppose not. And yet, one of the things I most admire in you, my dear, is your very ability to speak your mind."

Prudence surprised herself by saying, "I doubt very much you would appreciate my speaking my mind on this subject."

"Ah, so you *do* have an opinion. And one which I won't like, eh?" Ledbetter hesitated before he shrugged and said, "Tell me."

But Prudence's innate avoidance of the subject matter would not allow her to continue.

Ledbetter frowned. "How am I to know how to proceed if you won't speak up, Prudence? What is it you fear?"

She could do no more than shake her head.

"Very well. Let me see if I can straighten things out," He resisted her attempt to extract her hands from his grip. In fact, he shifted a little closer to her on the sofa so they would both be more comfortable with her hands in his. As he spoke, he absently rubbed her fingers. "Marriage. A man and a woman joining together to form a family. That would be my definition. Do you find that a satisfactory one?"

"Yes."

"Is there something you would add to it?"

Her shoulders lifted slightly. "I suppose not."

He regarded her with curious dark eyes. "When you were engaged to the young man in India . . ."

"Allen Porlonsby," she supplied.

"Right, Porlonsby. Perhaps then your definition would have included some statement of affection on the part of the participants, but that is scarcely a requirement in our society, is it?"

"No. I . . . no."

"So," he pushed on, "we have a man and a woman. Joining. I trust you understand how a man and a woman join together to produce children."

Prudence's throat felt dry, but she managed to say, "Yes, more or less."

"Ah, more or less. Would you like me to explain it to you?"

"No!"

"Would that be embarrassing?"

She tried again to retrieve her hands, but he held tightly to them. "Yes," she finally admitted.

"But you and I are wife and husband now," he protested.

"That doesn't make it any less embarrassing . . . or frightening."

"It should."

"How? Because a few words are spoken in front of us? Because we said 'I do'?" Prudence scoffed. "I scarcely know you, and yet I am to allow you to . . . to do with my body what you wish."

"Well, that's a part of marriage, that joining. That's how we will accomplish making a family." He regarded her with alarm. "You do wish to have children, don't you?"

"Of course I do!"

He smiled ruefully. "But there's no other way to create them, my dear. Trust me to be considerate of your sensibilities."

"My sensibilities! Oh, you don't understand at all."

Ledbetter was losing his patience. "What is it I don't understand, then? If you won't tell me, how shall I know?"

"How can you not know?" she declared indignantly. "How can you think that I would be so sanguine as to think nothing of having my body exposed to another, to a man I scarcely know? To have him touch it, to have him force his way into it? Oh, how can you not understand that?"

Her voice rang with despair, and Prudence fought to regain control. He was right, of course. This was what marriage was. He had every right to expect her to offer herself to him willingly. That is basically what she had promised when she married him, was it not?

She raised her head and met his astonished look. "Never mind," she said. "I understand my duty, and I'm prepared to do it."

"I daresay I should be grateful for that," he retorted. "You needn't be alarmed. I have no intention of forcing myself on you, Prudence."

# Chapter Six

Before he could say anything further, she hastened to interject an exclamation of alarm. "Oh, no, I know you would not! Please, Ledbetter, pay no heed to my missishness. It's just the nervousness of a woman who has achieved the age of two and twenty without marriage. I know what is expected of me! Oh, I knew it wasn't a good idea for me to say anything."

"I'm afraid it's a little late to take your words back, ma'am." Ledbetter rose and looked down on her. "Perhaps you could give me some idea of how long it will take you to accustom yourself to the idea of sharing a bed with me. Or have you taken me in such aversion that I am never to look forward to that husbandly situation?"

Prudence rose with all the dignity she could muster. "I would not have married you had I taken you in aversion, Ledbetter. What I have been trying to tell you is," she said, forcing the words through a constricted throat, "that I am a little shy where my . . . my body is concerned. Perhaps more than a little. And I am sorry for it, truly I am. All I ask is that you allow me a few days to . . . to steady my nerves."

"And how do you intend to do that?"

She could see that he was still angry, and she could not meet his gaze. "I will work at it," she promised.

"Nonsense." He gave an exasperated sigh and crossed to the mantel, where he stopped and regarded his wife for fully five minutes. At length he said, "It's like anything else one fears, Prudence. Avoiding the source of the fear only manages to increase it, to build it up in your mind. Last night you weren't sick, were you?"

"No." Her voice was so low that she wasn't sure if he could hear her. She cleared her throat and said a little louder, "No."

"And tonight you are even more fearful, aren't you?"

Tears glittered in her eyes but she kept her voice steady. "Perhaps a little."

"And tomorrow night it will be that much worse," he told her, scowling fearsomely. "Until you will be truly terrified and if I want to have an heir I'll have to kill you off and marry someone else."

Prudence, who had been sinking lower and lower into despair, realized that he was teasing and was able to laugh. "I hope the case may not become so desperate," she said, the tears gone from her eyes.

"That's better." He crossed the room and lifted her chin with a finger. "Here's what we'll do, if you can trust me a little. You'll share my bed, or I yours, as one of your sisters might. You understand?"

"Y-Yes."

"It is not my habit to wear anything to bed, but you needn't concern yourself with that."

"And I can wear a night dress?"

"Certainly. I trust you have some charming ones in your trunks."

"Several," she admitted.

"Very well." He tilted his head, his eyes questioning. "Do you think you can manage under those conditions?"

"Yes, but . . ."

"But?"

"How long can they last? How long are you prepared to wait?"

Ledbetter shrugged. "God knows. I am not a particularly patient man."

"I've noticed that," she said, a mischievous smile playing around her lips.

"Have you? And I have noticed that you are a rather headstrong woman. Not an especially felicitous combination, perhaps, but certainly a challenging one." He ran a finger along her cheek. "I'm going to kiss you now, Prudence."

Before anxiety could rise too high in her chest, she found his lips on hers. It was not the first time she had been kissed, of course. Allen had kissed her a number of times, and very sweetly, too. Ledbetter's kiss was not sweet at all. His arms came around her to pull her firmly against him and his mouth covered hers in a demanding sort of way, as though he expected something from her. The tentative brush of her lips had him pulling back and rolling his eyes in disgust.

"I'm not your mama," he told her. "That's the kind of kiss you might give her, or a sister who was going away to school. I'm your husband. Don't you know the difference?"

"No," she said frankly. "What other kind of kiss is there?"

"I'll demonstrate for you sometime," he assured her, setting her carefully aside. "Go and get ready for bed, my dear. I'll join you in half an hour."

"In my room?"

"Yes, in your room." He lifted her chin again and made her meet his gaze. "Remember what I've promised. There is not the slightest need for you to be frightened."

"Thank you."

When she had left the room, Ledbetter sighed and retrieved his brandy glass from the side table. With a mocking smile he lifted it heavenward. "To you, Porlonsby," he muttered. "Quite the gentleman you must have been. I suppose I look quite crass in comparison." He took a quick gulp of the rich amber liquid and returned the glass to the table.

For some time he stood staring into the fire, a slight frown lowering his brows. Then he absently kicked a log farther onto the fire, shrugged, and headed for his room.

Despite his promise, Prudence was nervous. She lay stiffly in her new bed, her most modest nightdress enveloping every inch of flesh from her chin to her ankles. When she had released the pins from her hair, it had sprung in all directions and she had ruthlessly brushed it into something like submission. But with her head on the pillow she could tell that her hair had fanned out around her head like a misbegotten halo. Ledbetter would think she looked like a witch.

She had left a candle burning, as on the previous night. Its flame wavered in the slight breeze that wafted through the room, casting long shadows on the walls and ceiling. Prudence had left the velvet hangings open on one side, where Ledbetter could climb into the bed. She herself had rolled as far as possible to the other side and waited there with her lips caught between her teeth.

There was a soft knock on her door, and she forced herself to say, "Come in." Ledbetter entered, in a royal blue dressing gown that sat easily on his broad shoulders. He set his candle down beside hers, and in the double light regarded her for a long moment. "You'll fall out of bed if you get any further over," he said dryly before snuffing both candles.

In the darkness Prudence saw him start to remove the dressing gown and she turned her gaze away, remembering what he had said about sleeping without clothes. She had taken pains to warm his side of the bed with a warming pan and hoped it had not cooled off before he arrived. Now she

felt the mattress shift as he positioned himself on his side of
the bed.

Hoping to sound perfectly normal, she said a cheerful
good night. His rumble of quiet laughter slightly shook the
bed. "My dear girl, we're not ready to go to sleep yet," he
said.

"We aren't?"

"No, we're going to talk for a few minutes. Give me your
hand."

"My hand?"

"Yes, dear. I'm going to hold your hand while we talk."

"Why?" She could tell when he reached a hand across toward her and she timidly placed hers in it.

"Because we need to have some physical contact." He
twined his fingers with hers and then began to rub his thumb
against her skin. "Tell me why your sister Lizzie would have
put whitewash in my shaving soap."

The question startled a laugh out of her. "Did she?
Naughty Lizzie. Did you catch her doing it?"

"Oh, no. But there is no one else who could possibly have
been responsible, and I saw her studying my face very carefully when I appeared for the marriage service."

"She must have been disappointed that you weren't white
as a sheep." Prudence smiled in the dark at the picture which
formed in her mind. Then a thought distracted her. "Did you
tell anyone?"

"No, of course not. I had no wish to get her in trouble. But
I was a little concerned that it might mean she had taken me
in dislike."

"I don't think so." Prudence remembered Lizzie's fears
about the marriage, but they hadn't really centered on Ledbetter. "She just can't resist playing pranks now and then.
And I don't think she was happy that I was leaving home."

"No, I don't think she was." He lifted her hand to his lips

and kissed it before returning it to the no-man's-land between them. "I told her she might visit us sometime."

Prudence was very aware that her arm had brushed along his bare chest when he lifted her hand to kiss it. This reminder that his body was naked made her stiffen slightly. "That was kind of you."

"Not particularly. She was offended that I didn't set a specific date."

"Poor Lizzie. She doesn't feel she has anything in common with my other two sisters, and indeed I cannot blame her."

"Hmm. No, you are very different from Elinor and Gladys. I received the impression neither of them share your shyness about your body."

Prudence felt her face flush in the dark. "Truly I am very sorry for it, Ledbetter."

"Don't apologize. I was merely remarking on the difference."

Prudence felt him shift on the bed at the same time he drew her hands closer to him. "Come, you're tired," he said. "Give me a kiss and I'll let you go to sleep."

His face was somehow very close to hers. Prudence leaned toward him and touched her lips briefly to his. "Again," he said, "for a little longer."

So she pressed her lips to his and allowed them to stay that way for a few moments. "Now let me show you," he suggested.

When his lips met hers, they were firm and had an urgency about them. They did not remain still, but seemed to seek out the corners and the fullness of her lower lip. And he wandered farther afield as well, nibbling at her chin and her nose and her closed eyes. By the time they returned to her mouth, Prudence was able to respond a bit more enthusiastically. Ledbetter at length drew back and said, "Yes, better. Good night, my dear. I hope you'll sleep well."

Relief flooded her. "I'm sure I shall. Good night, Ledbetter."

"Come, Prudence. It's time you called me by my given name."

"Yes, of course . . . William. I . . . I'm grateful for your patience."

"Just remember that I don't possess an inexhaustible supply."

"I will."

Prudence awoke in the morning to the sound of the draperies being pushed aside on their rod. Sunlight poured into the room, engulfing her even on the far side of the large bed. For a moment she thought it must be Ledbetter who had tossed them open, but a girl's voice spoke from behind the bed.

"His lordship asked me to bring your tea, Lady Ledbetter. Shall I put it on the dressing table?"

"Yes, thank you. Can you tell me what time it is?"

"Gone nine, milady. Shall I bring you some hot water?"

"Nine!" Prudence tossed back the covers and swung her feet to the floor. She could see the girl now, a young fresh-faced child who was regarding her with awe. "Yes, I would appreciate some hot water. I'm afraid I've forgotten your name."

"Betsy, ma'am." The child dropped a curtsy. "Mrs. Collins said I was to help you until your own maid came."

My own maid, Prudence thought. Ledbetter had no doubt already explained her impulsive act to the housekeeper. Well, what was done was done. And she didn't regret her action, just wondered whether it would have been wiser to wait until she'd gotten to Salston to choose someone. Ah, well.

By the time Betsy returned with the pitcher of hot water, Prudence was standing at the dressing table, sipping at the hot tea. And wondering what the routine at Salston was. Now there was something she could have discussed with Ledbetter, a subject of some import, but she very much doubted Ledbetter's patience ran to describing household matters. She would spend a few hours with Mrs. Collins instead, which would no doubt serve all of them a great deal better.

Prudence was accustomed to having an abigail assist in her dressing, but only with the occasional external touches. Four sisters sharing an abigail had not led her to depend on someone to help her in and out of her nightdress and her undergarments. And indeed her shyness extended to *anyone* seeing her unclothed, not just her new husband. So she asked Betsy to come back in quarter of an hour, when she would be ready for assistance with the impossible row of buttons on the back of the dress she planned to wear that day.

Before the quarter hour had expired, there was a tap on the door accompanied by Ledbetter's voice asking if it would be convenient for her to see him. Prudence's first impulse was to say "no," but as she had already stepped into her round gown, she offered a reluctant, "If you will wait but a moment." Quickly shrugging her arms through the sleeves, she adjusted the gown so that it covered her sufficiently before allowing her husband into the room.

"I trust you didn't mind my having tea sent up," he said as he strolled into the room. He was dressed in country garb, buckskin breeches and top boots, with a handsome brown riding jacket. "I did want to speak with you before I rode out."

"Of course. I had no intention of sleeping so late. At home I'm up much earlier."

"Yes, so you've said." His gaze drifted from her face to the mirror behind her, and he smiled. "Turn around. I'll do you up."

"That's not at *all* necessary," she protested, flushing. "Betsy will be back in just a few minutes."

"Turn around."

Prudence did as she was bid.

His hands came to rest on her shoulders, where they remained as he regarded the two of them in the mirror. "I hadn't realized how tall you were, Prudence," he remarked. "And in your stocking feet, too."

Prudence looked with chagrin at the stockings she had already pulled on. They were not new ones by any means. In fact she could see that the right one had been mended. There had seemed so many more important things to be taken care of in the short time she'd had before her wedding, that she'd ended up having to bring all the stockings she had owned for the last few years. Trust Ledbetter to notice.

For he had noticed. She could see that little quiver at the corner of his mouth, and the way his eyes almost teased her. Well, she would buy new stockings the first time they visited the village shops and in the meantime she would give any mended stockings to Betsy for a charity drive.

"If you would just do up my gown," she suggested with some asperity.

"Certainly, my dear." His fingers on the buttons were nimble and he was almost finished when Betsy arrived to assist his wife. The little maid looked surprised to see him there. She curtsied and offered to come back later but Prudence firmly stated that she was ready for Betsy's help with her hair.

Ledbetter reached up to place a hand on either side of Prudence's head, his fingers weaving into her thick auburn tresses. "You know, I'm of a mind to ask you to leave your hair down, Prudence. It's very becoming when it's loose, don't you think, Betsy?"

"Oh, yes, my lord. Lady Ledbetter looked ever so much like my school mistress yesterday with it all pulled back and pinned so tight."

"There," he said, smiling at her in the glass. "You don't wish to look like a school mistress, do you, Prudence?"

"Perhaps I would prefer that to looking like a green girl with my hair springing about with a mind of its own. Pinning it is the only way to gain some control over it."

"I like it loose." Ledbetter ran his fingers through her heavy mane of hair, making her almost shiver. "Controlling it seems such a shame. Would you, just for today, indulge me in this?"

Prudence sighed. "It is very odd of you. I shall present quite a slovenly appearance to your staff, sir." When he continued to regard her with raised brows, she said, "Oh, very well, if it is what you wish."

"Thank you, my dear." To her astonishment, and Betsy's delight, he placed a kiss on her nape. "I'm afraid I must be off now. Look for me in the early afternoon and we will make a visit to Sir Geoffrey Manning and his good lady to apprise them of my marriage. They are our closest neighbors and he is a lifelong friend of mine."

"I shall look forward to it," she said, though nothing could have been further from the truth. She did not feel ready to make the acquaintance of so old a friend of his, let alone appear before Lady Manning with her wild hair undone. She would wear a hat, she decided, which would sufficiently curb its excesses. Ledbetter could not complain of that. And, honestly, if he intended to dictate to her on matters of appearance, he would do well to think again.

When the baron had closed the door behind himself, Prudence seated herself at the dressing table and allowed Betsy to brush the tangles from her hair. With each stroke her hair seemed to stand out more from her head until it formed an amber nimbus. "You see," she complained. "It is absolutely unmanageable this way."

"But, my lady," Betsy protested, "it's the most beautiful hair I've ever seen!"

Startled, Prudence regarded herself dispassionately in the mirror. All her life she'd been used to thinking her hair a trial. From the age of twelve she had rigorously tortured it into obedience in a series of braids or twists which she pinned securely to her head. What she saw now was that her hair was very much like her sister Lizzie's, which she had always admired, in a girl that age. But to allow her own hair this wild freedom and she was a woman of two-and-twenty! Surely that must be unacceptable.

"Well, for today," she agreed, a frown settling on her brow. "But not to the Mannings. I will not have Sir Geoffrey and Lady Manning thinking me a heathen!"

# Chapter Seven

L edbetter firmly put his wife from his mind after he left her room. He had a great deal to take care of on his first day back at Salston. Already his estate manager had sent a list of items which he felt must be personally addressed by the baron. Then there were the two very specific matters that Ledbetter alone knew of. Now that he had sufficient funds, the sooner he put those demands behind him, the better.

His horse was already saddled when he arrived at the stables. They knew his ways there, and understood that every day after he breakfasted, he would appear for a gallop on Thor, unless some emergency held him back. Apparently the stable lads did not consider his marriage anything out of the ordinary, as Thor stomped impatiently when Ledbetter came into the stable yard.

The horse was magnificent. He had cost Ledbetter a great deal more than he should have paid, but once having set eyes on the black stallion, Ledbetter would not be satisfied until he owned him. It was his one regret when he was in London, that the stallion remained at Salston. But Thor was a high-strung beast and the one time Ledbetter had brought him to the metropolis, Thor had proved impossibly skittish in the hustle and bustle of the city. He had taken objection to every loud noise, had attempted to challenge half a dozen other stallions, and had proved nigh impossible to control in the park.

Thor was built to run and holding him in seemed almost a cruelty. As Ledbetter mounted now, he could feel the muscles tense in the powerful beast. With only a modest urging, Thur surged forward, his stride lengthening with almost impossible speed. Ledbetter gloried in the unfettered freedom of that gallop—across fields, over fences, around the lake. After two days in a carriage, and a night spent cursing himself for a fool, the baron fully appreciated the release of galloping madly across half of his estate before at length guiding Thor toward the village.

The stone church lay at the end of the main street of the village of Forstairs. There were only four streets, and three of them were better described as paths. But the main street was cobbled and well maintained, with shops lining both sides. From boy to man, Ledbetter had come to Forstairs with a certain anticipation, for despite its country aspect, there was one shop which invariably claimed his attention.

The pastry cooks stood next door to the modest inn, and supplied the inn with all manner of baked goods. But the Rules family who had owned it for generations were a truly remarkable group. Not even in London had Ledbetter found their match for scones and pastries and whimsical delicacies. He remembered being allowed as a boy to choose something from the wooden shelves, and how it had been almost an agony to have to pick one from the many wonderful treats.

As he passed on Thor, he waved to Mrs. Rule, who was standing in the doorway having a chat with the dry-goods clerk from down the way. She looked surprised at his passing by, but Ledbetter was determined to attend to business first. And business, in this instance, was the village church.

He dismounted close to the wooden doors with their heavy iron handles. The vicar might be in the building, or he might be in the vicarage, but Ledbetter preferred to investigate the church first. For one thing, he wished to see if his mother's instructions had been properly carried out. Though the day was reasonably bright outdoors, Ledbetter found the interior of the church as gloomy as it had always been. There were too few windows, and those there were contained murky glass which served only to smudge out any light attempting to reach the interior.

Still, there was sufficient light to see the organ. Ledbetter shook his head at the folly of it. It was a magnificent organ, with series upon series of pipes, a gleaming keyboard, an upholstered stool for the organist. But its size was totally disproportionate to the small church. No finer instrument could have been found in the entire county, despite the fact that there were churches ten times the size of that in Forstairs. Lord, Ledbetter thought, the sound must batter the eardrums of every congregant, to say nothing of the rest of the village.

And to what purpose? In a cathedral the organ might have given pleasure to its listeners. The hymns played on it might have uplifted the hearts and souls of worshippers. But here? In Forstairs? What could his mother have been thinking of?

"So, what do you think of our organ, Lord Ledbetter?" a voice behind him asked with a rather heavy Yorkshire accent.

Ledbetter composed his features before turning to face the vicar. "I think it is entirely too large for the church, Mr. Hidgely."

The vicar regarded him with surprise. "But it is what your mama wished, sir. She was quite explicit in her will."

"Yes, she was," the baron agreed after a thoughtful pause. "Surprisingly explicit, I have always thought."

"But then dear Lady Ledbetter was a very active member of the church, though the rest of her family has not always followed her lead. For many years she had wished to see the old organ replaced. She made quite a study of organs during her last year."

All very true, unfortunately. Ledbetter had found information about organs in half the drawers in his mother's desk. She had, it appeared, become quite obsessed with them during her last months. There were replies from manufacturers and London organists answering questions she had obviously posed to them. And he knew for a fact that she enjoyed organ music. But this—this huge organ was a travesty. Surely she had known that the small village church needed a much smaller instrument.

"A great pity that her study had such an unfortunate result." Ledbetter reached into the inside pocket of his coat and extracted an envelope. "You will find the balance of the funds covered by this draft, Mr. Hidgely. Though I don't myself believe it was necessary to interpret my mother's legacy as encompassing the rebuilding of that portion of your church which had formerly housed the old organ, I won't quibble with your having done so."

"We could not very well have got such a large instrument inside without rebuilding, my lord," the vicar protested. He surreptitiously inspected the figure on the draft and smiled. "We have done precisely what your sainted mother wished, and accomplished it in the year since her death, as she requested. I trust you will be attending the dedication on Sunday."

Ledbetter was tempted to offer an excuse, but knew better than to do so. "Yes, I'll be here—with my wife."

Mr. Hidgely frowned. "Your wife? I had no idea you had married. My felicitations, of course."

"Thank you." Ledbetter took one last look at the organ before turning to leave. "Sunday, then, Hidgely. I trust you have found someone to play it."

"Indeed, my lord. A most exceptional young man. We are truly lucky to have found someone so talented."

"Excellent."

Ledbetter nodded to the vicar and made his way from the gloomy church into the light of day. Thor waited impatiently where the baron had left him, but instead of springing onto his mount, Ledbetter took hold of his reins and led him up the street. "I need to get *some* pleasure from this visit," he muttered, tying his horse in front of the Rules' shop.

Ledbetter's second errand had proved no more satisfactory than his first, and by the time he arrived back at Salston he was in an irritable frame of mind. His marriage was so new to him, and so preoccupied was he with the frustrations of the morning, that he was literally startled to discover Prudence arranging flowers in a vase in the Great Hall.

He had come through a side door, where he had left his muddy boots, and proceeded in stocking feet through the small parlor and into the hall. Because he made no sound whatsoever, his wife didn't hear him enter, and he was able to observe her unaware for several minutes.

As promised, she had left her hair unbound and it made a glorious cloud around her head. The dress he had buttoned that morning fit her figure well, and not for the first time he remarked on what a fine figure it was. She hummed to herself, her deft fingers working the blossoms into a clever arrangement. She looked for all the world as though she'd been at Salston for years, and was quite happy to be there.

"My dear," he said softly, so as not to startle her, "Mrs. Collins has already put you to work, has she?"

"Hardly. If I had nothing to do, I should be bored to death. Have you lost your boots, Led . . . William?"

"Just obeying an old rule of my mother's never to track

mud into the house. I suppose, being master of the place, I could track mud where I like, but old habits die hard."

"Thank heaven. If you've been in the stable yard, it's not just mud your boots would be tracking in."

He moved closer to her, and captured one of her hands, which he lifted to his mouth to kiss. "You look the picture of domesticity, Prudence. Have you spent the morning familiarizing yourself with Salston?"

She watched a little nervously as he raised the other hand to his lips. "Yes. Mrs. Collins gave me a thorough tour this morning. There are a number of matters I wish to discuss with you, but there is no urgency about any of them. Did you have a good ride?"

"The ride was fine." He pulled her toward himself and would have kissed her, but a footman appeared in the doorway to announce that the light collation my lady had ordered was available in the breakfast parlor. Prudence took the opportunity to loosen her hands from his grip as she turned to the footman. "Thank you, Gibbons. I'll be along in a moment."

When she turned back to him, she looked a little hesitant. "Will you wish to change before you eat, William?"

"I had something in Market Stotton. You go ahead. I'll change into something to wear to the Mannings'."

"You've been to Market Stotten? But that's a good fifteen miles away, is it not?"

"Twelve. I had business there." And being reminded of it served to rouse his temper again. He turned away from her. "I'll be ready to leave by two."

"Very well."

Prudence chose her emerald velvet bonnet, because it served to tame her hair as well as matching the trim of her gown. She was ready and waiting in the front parlor when

Ledbetter appeared at precisely two o'clock. When he saw her, he smiled appreciatively.

"Fetching, my dear. Green suits you very well."

Prudence dropped a shy curtsy. "Thank you, my lord."

He tucked her arm inside his and led her toward the hall. "The Mannings live about half a mile away, so I thought we'd take the phaeton. I was tempted to surprise them with my news, but thought better of it."

"You sent a message ahead, then?"

"Yes, informing them that I would be bringing my bride to visit."

Prudence glanced up at his face but she couldn't read anything of significance there. "They must have been astonished to hear that you had married."

"Probably, but all Geoffrey wrote back was: 'We'll be here.'"

"A man of few words."

Ledbetter looked thoughtful. "Yes, I suppose he is. With a very sweet wife, his childhood sweetheart. I think we have both known Catherine all our lives. They've been married forever, and have a number of children. I don't remember how many precisely. Catherine's forever increasing."

Prudence felt color rush to her face. He hadn't said it to distress her, she knew, so she fought to overcome her discomfort. "I imagine you are godfather to at least one of them," she suggested.

"Why, no, they've never done me that honor." Apparently this struck him as somewhat unusual, now the thought had been put in his mind. "I daresay it is because I am so much in London."

"No doubt." To change the subject, she said, "And how long has your sister been married?"

"Oh, Harriet met Markham at her come-out. That must be four years ago. She married him that very summer." Ledbetter halted abruptly in the hallway just as a footman was opening the front door for them. "But she's godmother to one of the Mannings' children, and she doesn't even live in the county anymore. What do you make of that?"

"I imagine she is a very close friend of Lady Manning."

"Well, she is, but I am a very close friend of both of them." Ledbetter started walking again, but a decided frown had gathered on his brow.

"It may be only that you were a single man," Prudence offered by way of explanation. "Perhaps they thought you would not wish for the responsibility."

"Ha! More like they did not wish for my bad influence," he muttered.

They had reached the phaeton and Ledbetter assisted Prudence onto the high seat. All things considered, she would have preferred a closed carriage, but Ledbetter had really not offered her a choice. She imagined he preferred to drive himself when he could, and when the weather looked promising.

Ledbetter sprang up beside her and gathered the reins from the stable lad who had been holding them. But he hesitated then, cocking his head toward her. "Are you going to be warm enough, Prudence? That redingote looks a little thin for a drive. Ah, you thought we would be taking the chaise, didn't you?"

"I'll be fine."

Ledbetter regarded her ruefully. "I hope there is not a streak of the martyr in you, my dear, for I'm so accustomed to doing precisely as I please that I probably won't even notice your sacrifices."

Prudence laughed. "I can well believe it. But what are my options, sir? If I make you wait for me to go in and search out a heavier garment, you will be impatient. If I suggest that we change carriages, you will be exasperated with me, and the delay will be even longer. I fear my first answer was the correct one. I shall be fine."

"I suppose I *would* be impatient, but you will learn to pay no heed to that. My sister does not. In fact, I cannot think when she's been ready on time, even for church. I admit I was inordinately pleased to find you waiting for me just now. Here," he said, handing her the reins, "I'll run in and get one of Harriet's heavy shawls from the side room. She leaves one there for taking walks when she visits."

Prudence accepted the reins without fear, as the groom still stood at the horses' heads. Her husband sprang down from the carriage and bounded up the stairs and into the house. His was such a fine, athletic figure that she could not help but admire it—from a distance. He was gone no more than three minutes, and returned carrying a blue woolen shawl which had seen better days. He grimaced as he placed it around her shoulders.

"I'm afraid it's a bit disreputable, to say nothing of not matching your charming outfit. But it will surely keep you warm, and if you are so inclined, you may remove it before we drive up to Sir Geoffrey's door."

"An excellent idea," she murmured. "I find it difficult to picture Harriet wearing it."

"Well, I may be wrong about how long it has been since she did so. You know how things seem to accumulate in mud rooms—old boots, and heavy stockings, and sweaters and caps. When I took the shawl down from the hook I found under it a cap of mine that I had thought long gone. Quite a favorite of mine, when I was a boy. I daresay you'll want to have some of that aging mess cleared out."

"Probably. I'm a tidy soul at heart."

He had given the horses the signal to start and they stepped out briskly. Prudence was a little surprised at how high she was from the ground. She wrapped one hand securely around the bar at her side. Ledbetter's attention was on his horses, but he asked, "Have you ridden in a high-perch phaeton before?"

"No."

"It takes some getting used to. You needn't be alarmed, though. I'm a fairly skilled driver, if I say so myself."

"I'm glad to hear it," she said as they bounced over a rut in the road. "One certainly does get a bird's eyes view from this height."

"Much more interesting than the view from a curricle," Ledbetter assured her. "All you see are hedgerows from a curricle, miles and miles of greenery without any distant prospect. Geoffrey and I argue the merits of the high perch versus the curricle all the time."

"So even with a large family Sir Geoffrey races about the countryside in a curricle, does he?"

Ledbetter cast her a brief glance. "Do I detect a note of disapproval, my dear? Perhaps you believe that a gentleman should become quite staid upon his marriage."

"No, I believe that a gentleman should do his best not to break his neck when he has a family."

"Ah, well, Geoffrey isn't going to break his neck in a curricle. I'm more likely to do that in the phaeton."

"So I would imagine." But she smiled a little shyly at him and said, "Actually I find it quite exhilarating."

"Do you? Good girl. Shall I have them pick up the pace a bit?"

"No, thank you. This is exciting enough for me."

Ledbetter laughed and kept a steady hand on the reins. Even when his horses were startled by a pair of pheasants erupting from the roadside bushes, he exerted a fine control over them. Prudence relaxed a little beside him, enjoying the view of her new county. Fields stretched off on either side of the lane, and the occasional cottage sprang up on the horizon. Birds wheeled overhead and there was birdsong from the bushes. Rolling hills bore patches of trees that would soon bud into spring greenery. And after a while a larger house came into view. Its gray stone walls sprawled over an immense courtyard.

"The Mannings' place," Ledbetter said. "Hawthorne Manor. I spent half my youth here."

There was a wistfulness to his voice that surprised Prudence. Somehow one did not expect Lord Ledbetter to concern himself with his younger days, before he had grown to manhood. Still, it was easy enough for her to picture him here, darting about the courtyard with his friend, taking off to fish in the nearby stream, racing horses along the boundary walls.

As the phaeton drew closer to the buildings, Prudence allowed the shawl to slide down her back onto the seat of the carriage. Meeting Ledbetter's oldest friends would be difficult enough without being seen to arrive in a shabby woolen shawl. This way the Mannings would only think her very strange for having driven so far in a flimsy redingote.

# Chapter Eight

Ledbetter had spent some of the happiest hours of his youth at Hawthorne Manor. He had found in Geoffrey a kindred spirit, someone who was as intent on sowing his wild oats as Ledbetter himself. Sir John Manning and his wife had been the kind of parents any young man could have wished for, always loving and wise in their guidance of their children, and of Ledbetter, too.

And Martha Manning. Two years younger than Geoffrey and himself, a beautiful and spirited girl, she had been his first love. Ledbetter had assumed that he would marry her, as Geoffrey eventually married Catherine. But he had lost himself in London's many pleasures and, if not forgotten her, then lost the urgency he had felt about making a life with her. The appeal of domesticity had entirely deserted him when he discovered that being a single man in the metropolis offered so many temptations.

They hadn't had an understanding, he and Martha. Sir John had with his usual frankness insisted that they were both too young to make any commitment. And this had relieved Ledbetter when he indulged in the delights of gaming and boxing and attending masquerades and, eventually, taken a mistress. Quite a man of the world, he had not been prepared for the letter from Geoffrey announcing his sister's engagement.

At first Ledbetter had been stunned. He had always seen

Martha as waiting for him in the background. Whenever he visited home, and Hawthorne Manor, there she was, as vivacious and pretty as he remembered. Each time he had considered offering for her, but had put off the actual deed for one reason or another. Still, he was always convinced that she loved him.

And so, when Geoffrey announced her engagement, Ledbetter felt sure that she had either done it to galvanize him, or out of a fear that he would never come up to scratch. In either case, he knew that he needed to see her and assure her of his continued attachment. So, he had gone haring off to Hampshire, intent on setting matters right. Fortunately, he happened to witness a revealing scene between Martha and her fiancé before he could make a complete fool of himself. It was quite obvious to Ledbetter when he watched them that they were in love, and he was surprised by the enormity of the loss he felt.

But that was a long time ago, Ledbetter thought as he handed Prudence down from the phaeton. Martha had been married for the better part of ten years, he supposed, and she was the mother of several children. Sir John had died and his wife had moved to live with her sister so that Geoffrey and Catherine and their children alone occupied Hawthorne Manor.

Ledbetter knew that his blunt announcement of his marriage would have surprised, and perhaps worried, Geoffrey and Catherine. He stole a glance at his wife as she allowed the butler to relieve her of her redingote. Though not perhaps in the first blush of youth, she was a fine looking woman. In fact, her countenance seemed more attractive to him now than it had when she'd had her London Season four years ago. He repressed a smile as she gave up her bonnet with obvious reluctance.

He realized she had depended on the bonnet to press her

hair into submission but that magnificent hair, no longer trapped under the confining confection, sprang to life. Ledbetter would have buried his fingers in it had they been alone. As the butler turned to announce them, Ledbetter possessed himself of Prudence's hands, which were making ineffectual attempts to tame her tresses. "You look fine," he assured her, tucking her hand through his arm. "Come and meet my friends."

He paused for but a moment on the threshold of the room, to take in the sight before him. Geoffrey and Catherine and two of their children were seated on the floor playing jackstraws. Catherine was again increasing, Ledbetter saw, with probably only a month to await the new arrival.

Geoffrey sprang to his feet at the butler's announcement of them and turned to assist his wife. The children darted across the room, calling, "Uncle Will, Uncle Will!" But they stopped short at the sight of an unfamiliar woman and studied Prudence with undisguised curiosity.

"This is my wife, Lady Ledbetter," he told them. "Come and shake her hand, John, Clarissa, and tell her how old you are, because she will want to know and I'm sure I can never remember."

John, a tall and spindly child, stepped forward and extended a hand to Prudence. "How do you do, Lady Ledbetter?" he said with exaggerated politeness. "I'm John, and I'm eight."

"How do you do," Prudence replied solemnly as she shook his hand. When his sister, shorter and rounder, with a bevy of curls around her face, approached Prudence, she extended her hand, saying, "And you are Clarissa. How do you do?"

"Very well, my lady." The child blinked shyly. "I'll be six next week."

"Next week? My congratulations."

Sir Geoffrey made a shooing motion with his hands. "Off with you now, children. Your mama and I wish to make Lady Ledbetter's acquaintance with a measure of peace."

The two giggled and raced each other from the room. Sir Geoffrey extended a hand to Prudence and welcomed her kindly. Then he turned a rueful grin on Ledbetter. "You've managed to surprise us, Will. We had no idea you were thinking of marriage."

"No, indeed," his wife agreed, coming forward to clasp Prudence's hand. "How delightful to meet you, Lady Ledbetter. Welcome to Hawthorne Manor."

"Thank you."

Prudence accepted the chair Sir Geoffrey indicated, but Ledbetter felt too restless to sit. He moved behind his wife's chair, and placed a hand on her shoulder. "Prudence is a Stockworth, from Hampshire. We originally met four years ago when she made her come-out in London."

"Four years ago?" Lady Manning exclaimed. "How extraordinary!"

Sir Geoffrey regarded his old friend with amusement. "And it took you all this time to win her hand? I'm surprised at you, Will."

Ledbetter saw that in attempting to give himself some history with Prudence he'd merely fallen into a trap. "Alas, four years ago she paid not the least attention to me. We have only recently renewed our acquaintance."

"It sounds very romantic," Lady Manning assured her guest. "You'll take tea with us, won't you, Lady Ledbetter?"

"Thank you, yes. You have other children, I believe, for we saw some faces peering out the window above."

"Our fifth is on the way. Two girls and two boys."

As the women drifted into talk of the young ones, Ledbetter moved toward the windows, where Geoffrey joined him. "I felicitate you, Will," his friend said, but he looked troubled. He was a sturdily built man with sandy hair and piercing blue eyes. "When I saw you a month ago, I don't believe you had any thoughts of marrying."

"It was certainly not something I spoke of then." Ledbetter glanced over to where the women were cheerfully talking. "Past time I was married. Harriet came for the nuptials, but had to go directly back to London."

This piece of information seemed to mollify Geoffrey somewhat. "I trust Harriet is well."

"Extremely. About to launch Markham's sister, though, and she seemed to think that preparing for the ball could be delayed long enough to venture only briefly to Colwyck."

Geoffrey shook his head wonderingly. "I know she loves the social whirl of London as much as you do. Don't understand it myself."

Ledbetter laughed. "I know you don't. But we aren't all meant to rusticate the way you do." A grim thought thinned his lips. "I stopped at the church this morning."

"That damned organ," Geoffrey muttered. "Ludicrous, ain't it? Did you see Hidgely?"

"Yes, and spoke with him. He expects us at the dedication Sunday. I have a mind not to show up."

His friend shook his head. "Wouldn't do that, Will. Almost a memorial to your mother. Folks would think you were spurning her memory."

"The devil! If I thought it was possible to get to the bottom of this . . ." Ledbetter very nearly ground his teeth.

A footman arrived bearing the tea tray. As always it was loaded to overflowing with biscuits and cakes, bread and butter, everything to tempt indulgence. Geoffrey gave him a sympathetic look and urged him back toward the ladies. "No sense crying over spilled milk," he growled.

Only when Prudence glanced up at him and looked worried did Ledbetter realize he was still scowling. He forced himself to smile at her and say, "It's a tradition here to stuff one's visitors so they won't need another meal for two days."

Catherine laughed and shook her head. "I *think* the tradition developed when Will used to visit as a lad, Lady Ledbetter," she confided. "My mama-in-law did not believe they fed him well enough at Salston, for he was forever eyeing the cakes as though he were desperately hungry."

"Pure invention," Ledbetter scoffed. "Geoffrey's mama liked nothing better than to hear about our adventures, and the only way she could entice us to sit still long enough to relate them was to feed us macaroons. Isn't that true, Geoffrey?"

"I remember her laughing until the tears came," Geoffrey admitted as he helped himself to a biscuit. "Does it still when she visits and listens to John's tales."

Ledbetter gave him a searching look. "Do you expect her at Hawthorne anytime soon?"

"She'll come when the new babe arrives," Geoffrey said.

"Which could be any day from the looks of it," Ledbetter retorted.

"Another two weeks, possibly." Catherine held out a cup and saucer to Prudence. "They're almost always early."

"I'd like to talk with her, if I'm still here when she comes," Ledbetter said absently.

Three pairs of startled eyes turned toward him. "Why wouldn't you be here?" Geoffrey asked. "I thought you'd be situated at Salston for some time."

Ledbetter was particularly struck by the look on Prudence's face. She looked almost as though he'd repudiated her there in front of his friends. "I beg your pardon!" he exclaimed, wanting to reach out to reassure her but feeling it would be inappropriate to do so. "Of course I shall he here when your mama is. I have a rather urgent business matter to take care of, but that should see me away from Salston for no more than a few days. Lady Manning will surely be here for several weeks."

"Oh, yes," Catherine said. "Probably for a month or better."

"Well, then," Ledbetter assured his companions, "there shall be not the least difficulty."

The enjoyment of the visit which had previously been apparent in his bride had been extinguished, however. Though she continued to converse with her host and hostess, she had become distracted and Ledbetter could not doubt that he was entirely to blame. To make up for his careless error, he began to relate anecdotes from their younger years that he thought would interest his wife. Prudence smiled where appropriate but the haunted look did not disappear from her eyes.

He expected her to take him to task the moment they were in the carriage, but she said nothing. Even when they were far enough away from Hawthorne Manor that she pulled the old shawl up around her shoulders, she had not a word to say for herself. Ledbetter regarded her with a frown.

"My dear Prudence, I could tell what I said about being away upset you. I assure you I had not the least intention of doing so."

"You hadn't mentioned going away."

"No, well, I'm not certain when it will be yet."

"Nor for how long?"

Ledbetter distrusted the bland tone of her voice. "Nor for how long, but I trust it won't be more than a few days, as I told Geoffrey."

Prudence turned a steady gaze on him. "Do you know, William, that when you made that remark, it sounded very much as though you intended to simply depart, leaving me alone at Salston for an indefinite time."

Conflicting emotions tugged at him. She was his bride, and he had no wish to destroy any rapport building between them, but he was also his own man, marriage or no. His autonomy got the upper hand and he asked coolly, "Should you mind that very much? It seems to me that you might rather I weren't around to . . . make demands of you."

She flinched at this thrust and Ledbetter cursed under his breath. With great strength he drew his pair in to a stand, and turned to her. "That was unkind of me. And disingenuous. You must realize, Prudence, that I am not in the habit of consulting anyone about my comings and goings. I admit that I had rather thought to establish you at Salston and then be off about my usual pursuits."

"You might have mentioned that to me," she said in a strangled voice.

He put a finger under her chin to lift her face. "You must tell me what you want, and I will see if I can't accommodate you."

She shook her head. "It doesn't matter."

"Of course it matters," he said, his impatience obvious. "You don't want me to leave you alone at Salston, is that correct?"

"Yes."

"So would you prefer to come with me to London, or that I stay at Salston with you?"

"It doesn't matter."

"How can it not matter? Surely you have a preference."

Prudence gripped the shawl tightly about her shoulders and said, "The point is that I do not wish to be deserted."

"Deserted?" Ledbetter's brows drew down in a fierce scowl. "I have no intention of deserting you, Prudence. Just of coming and going between here and London as I've always done. Is it that you wish to spend time in London? That could be arranged."

"You don't understand," she insisted. "I would find it humiliating for you to walk away from me so soon after our marrying."

"Dear heaven, I'm not walking away from you." Ledbetter raked a gloved hand through his hair. "You cannot expect me to sit in your pocket!"

"I expect nothing of the sort. Never mind. Drive on, William. It's far too cold to keep your horses standing while we talk."

This at least was true. Ledbetter ground his teeth and gave a brisk slap of the reins to put the pair in motion. The abrupt movement of the phaeton nearly dislodged Prudence from her seat, but Ledbetter's arm swept out to hold her tightly in place. "Beg pardon," he apologized between his teeth.

His wife merely sighed.

Mrs. Collins had been a great help to Prudence in choosing the evening meal. She was, of course, familiar with all Ledbetter's likes and dislikes so far as dishes were concerned. And though Prudence intended over time to introduce a few dishes with which the cook was not as yet familiar, she thought it proper to delay the start of such an effort for a few weeks. Therefore, the meal that was put before Ledbetter that evening contained only those items which were sure to please him. And Prudence made every attempt to be a conversable companion.

"Mrs. Collins mentioned that there will be a dedication at the church on Sunday," she said, smiling at her husband across the length of the gleaming table. "Apparently your mother instructed that there be a fine organ placed there in her memory."

It had seemed to Prudence that this was more than a safe topic for discussion. And yet, her husband's face became instantly stormy, his eyes flashing, his lips pressed together, his brows fiercely lowered. For some time he said nothing and she knew not how to bridge whatever chasm she had opened. So she said nothing, but waited for him to explain his distress.

"Has Mrs. Collins seen the organ?" he eventually asked.

Prudence looked puzzled. "Seen it? Why, I have no idea. Ledbetter, whatever is the problem?"

"It's far too complicated to explain."

Her brows rose. "Really? I'm surprised to hear that. I should think I will need to know if there is something amiss."

Irritably Ledbetter dismissed the footman who was waiting on them. "It's not something I wish to be common knowledge," he said. "Naturally, in a town as small as Forstairs, everyone knows that my mother arranged in her will for an organ to be contributed to the church."

"Well, on the face of it, William, it sounds a very generous thing to do."

"Oh, indeed it was generous." His fingers drummed the table beside his plate. "Mother was quite specific about which organ was to be donated, as she had sent for information from a number of manufacturers. For whatever reason, and I'm sure I have not even a guess as to what the reason might be, she chose the largest, most expensive organ available."

"But such an organ would scarcely fit in a country church," Prudence protested.

"Precisely. The damn thing takes up half the building and will probably drive everyone out with the magnitude of its sound."

Prudence giggled. Ledbetter frowned at her. She covered her mouth with her hand, but the image of an organ of such size had struck her as immensely amusing. Despite her attempts to stifle her laughter, little gulps of it escaped past her hand and tinkled in the air between the two of them. She had an especially engaging laugh, did Prudence Stockworth Ledbetter. It rippled from her, unchecked after her initial attempts.

"Oh, I can scarcely wait to see it," she managed to say between gulps of laughter. "How ridiculous! How marvelous! Oh, may I go tomorrow to see it?"

"It's no laughing matter," Ledbetter growled.

"But it is! It's the funniest thing I've heard in weeks!"

"You lead a very dull life, then," he declared, but her laughter was infectious and the corners of his mouth had begun to twitch. "They had to take the church apart to get it in," he said.

Prudence laughed harder. "How wonderfully absurd!" she gasped.

"They're expecting me, us, at the dedication on Sunday," he told her. "If you're going to laugh like this, I'm not going to take you."

But he had at last allowed himself to succumb to the humor of the situation and shook his head as he joined in her amusement. Prudence dabbed at her tears with her serviette and drew long breaths to bring herself to a more sober contemplation of the problem.

"Well," she said at length, "I can see that it's a ridiculous situation, but I suspect there is more to it, if you are so concerned. Tell me what distresses you, William."

# Chapter Nine

"Aside from the inordinate, and useless, expense?" he grumbled.

"Yes, aside from that."

He hesitated for so long that Prudence realized he could not bring himself to confide in her. She had actually begun to eat again when he said, "I dislike our neighbors having such tangible evidence of my mother's folly."

"And perhaps that they might think it was your own folly?" she asked carefully.

He made an irritable gesture with one hand. "Oh, the vicar seems to have made it clear that the organ was bequeathed by my mother in her will."

"I'm surprised that you weren't able to find some way to prevent the folly from being carried through."

Ledbetter nodded. "Precisely. You would think in my position I would be able to bring the matter off satisfactorily, wouldn't you? Arrange for them to receive a smaller organ, earmark the remainder of the funds to some other worthy church project. A simple matter. But the vicar wouldn't have it. He wanted *this* organ, by God."

"Which makes you look impotent."

Ledbetter brooded on the word for a moment before grudgingly agreeing. "I even took both matters to court, but on this her will was upheld to the letter."

Prudence's brows rose. "Both matters?"

His face became shuttered, and he turned the subject. "I should like to give a dinner to introduce you to our neighbors, Prudence. Would that be asking too much of a new bride?"

She looked rueful. "How soon did you intend to give it?"

"Say, in a week or two. Nothing really elaborate, just dinner and dancing for a dozen couples."

"Oh, nothing elaborate." Her eyes danced. "I do love the way a man views these occasions."

"If it would be too much . . ." he said stiffly.

"I'm sure that with Mrs. Collins's help I can contrive." She set down her fork and leaned a little toward him. "You're not doing it because of what I said this afternoon, are you?"

"This afternoon?" He looked blank. "I don't recall your discussing a dinner."

Prudence sighed. "No indeed. Such a possibility would never have occurred to me."

"But it pleases you?"

"Why, yes. It does."

"Good." He offered her a slow smile, his eyes intent on her face. "I want to please you."

He had an odd way of showing it, she thought. But the timbre of his voice and the look in his eyes conveyed a message which made her pulse quicken. He was not talking about the dinner now. Well, she was perfectly capable of ignoring his subtle hints and discussing the many details necessary for her to arrange a dinner, and she proceeded to do so.

Ledbetter answered all her questions with unusual equanimity. But she detected a touch of amusement in the way his eyes crinkled and the corners of his mouth twitched. And she was aware, not for the first time, of a kind of *strength* about him. His hands, for instance, looked strong; she was reminded of the effort he had exerted with them that day to draw his team in. They were not necessarily gentle hands, like Allen's.

Allen's hands had been long and shapely, and very white. Ledbetter's were browned from the sun even this early in the year, and the black hair on their backs seemed to bristle. His fingers, curving around his wineglass, seemed alive with energy. Probably just with impatience, she reminded herself.

But she suddenly wondered how they would feel if they touched her, and the thought was so startling, and so alarming, that she flushed.

"Is something the matter?" he asked, angling his head slightly.

"Nothing," she assured him. "I should leave you to your port."

"You haven't finished your meal, Prudence."

"I've eaten everything I wish to. Truly."

Ledbetter looked doubtful, but he rose and came around the table to hold her chair, as he had sent the footman away. Before she could rise, he put a hand on her shoulder to stay her. "That portrait of my mother," he said, indicating the painting on the side wall, "was done when she was just your age. She'd already been married for five years, and I wasn't born for another three."

"She was a beautiful woman," Prudence said. His hand remained on her shoulder and she looked at him questioningly.

"Yes, she was, but very retiring even when she was young. I should like to think that you are more given to society than Mother was. I'm inclined to enjoy entertaining, and I hope it won't prove a burden to you."

"I shouldn't think it would, William." The longer his hand stayed on her shoulder, the more restless she became. "We did a considerable amount of entertaining at Colwyck, and as the oldest daughter the preparations were largely my province."

When Ledbetter finally raised his hand from her shoulder, he moved it to her hair. Prudence found herself holding her breath as he allowed his fingers to comb through her wild tresses. "Such glorious hair," he murmured. "And you wanting to hide it under a bushel."

"Hardly that," she objected. "Just to control it a little with pins."

"To what purpose?"

"Why, so that it won't look unkempt. When it is loose this way it looks wild and abandoned."

"Ah, perhaps that's why I like it this way," he teased, bringing his fingers down to trace the oval of her face. "It gives you that disheveled look of a woman just risen from her bed."

Prudence flushed under his gaze. "That is not a look to which I aspire, my lord."

He laughed. "Pity."

"I'll leave you to your port," she murmured, inching past him as he continued to partially block her way.

"Very well. I'll be along shortly."


Ledbetter actually stayed for some time in the dining room, sipping at a very tolerable port his father had laid down three decades previously. His father's portrait hung on the wall opposite his mother's, and he lifted his glass to it. "Hell of a cellar you assembled," he toasted. "A shame we can't get more from France these days."

The painting of his father had been done when the seventh baron was well into his middle years. Ledbetter supposed that earlier his father hadn't been willing to sit still long enough. The most vivid memory he had of his father was of a bruising rider gloriously charging across the north meadow at the head of the local hunt.

The seventh baron had had an excess of energy and drive, and an outgoing personality that was decidedly overbearing. That force was evident even in his chin and the high color in his face. Ledbetter had inherited the piercing blue eyes but none of the other characteristics that so distinguished his father's appearance.

And, of course, he'd inherited the impatience his father had frequently displayed. Not surprising, perhaps, since he had been subjected to it from his earliest years. And since it held no terrors for him. His mother, on the other hand, had been too timid to view such impatience with anything less than alarm. A quick, impatient word had frequently reduced her to tears, which always left the seventh baron puzzled and edgy. "What is it?" he would demand, in a booming voice, not helping the situation one whit.

Though Ledbetter recognized the same impatience in himself, he counted himself lucky not to possess his father's stentorian tones. Given his position, people jumped to do his bidding, and there was never the least need to raise his voice. He had, in fact, learned the value of keeping a very civil tongue, and therefore he was always a little surprised when someone, usually his sister, called him on his impatience.

"It is the *tone* of your voice," Harriet would insist. "There is that about it which I cannot like, as though you are angry with me."

And Ledbetter would reply, "Nonsense! You have altogether too much sensibility, Harriet! No one is angry with you."

Ledbetter certainly was not angry with his wife. But he was most decidedly impatient for more physical contact with her. He contemplated the last sip of port in his glass with a baleful eye. At the rate things were progressing, it would be a year before he managed to see her naked!

And he had a real desire to see her naked.

Ledbetter polished off the last of his port, decided against pouring himself another glass, and rose from the table.

Well, he would do his level best to move the seduction of his wife forward. He was not, he believed, an incompetent where charming women were concerned. He had, after all, spent a great deal of time in London and much of that time he'd had some woman or other in keeping. Jenny in particular had been insistent that he pay attention to her needs as well as his own, which had been something of a revelation to Ledbetter.

He strolled into the Gold Drawing Room with his most winning smile firmly fixed on his face—only to find that his wife was not there. "Devil take her!" he muttered. After making a close inspection of the room for some hint of where Prudence had disappeared to, and finding nothing, he stepped back out into the hall and motioned to the footman stationed in the entry hall.

"Do you know where Lady Ledbetter has gone?"

"Her ladyship said to tell you, if you asked, that she would be back shortly, my lord."

And I'm supposed to just cool my heels, am I? he thought, chagrined. Prudence was proving a great deal more trouble than he'd thought she would be. She had always struck him as a sensible girl, even when he'd met her during her Season. In fact, if that callow youth Porlonsby hadn't moved in with such surprising speed to win her, Ledbetter had intended to get to know the young woman better himself. Another lesson in carelessness for him.

Ledbetter waited impatiently in the Gold Drawing Room for quarter of an hour. He knew he had waited quarter of an hour because the ormolu clock on the mantel chimed when he first sat down, and again as he was rising to pace about the room. Once he was on his feet, he decided that he was going to wait no longer, but go to find out what had become of his errant wife. Ledbetter was not in the habit of waiting for anyone.

It seemed most likely that she had gone to her room, so he picked up a candle and headed in that direction. But perhaps she had needed to use the facilities, he thought, slowing his pace as he made his way up the stairs and down the hall. There was a water closet next to her room, but the door was open slightly and he could see that there was no one in it. On the other hand, the door to her room was closed and he heard the murmur of voices beyond it.

He rapped sharply on her door and the voices stopped abruptly. After a moment, Prudence's hesitant voice called, "Ledbetter?"

"Yes, of course it's me," he said irritably. "Is there something the matter?"

"I intend to join you shortly."

"So I was told some while ago. May I come in?"

"No!"

There was a hurried whispering, and then the maid Betsy opened the door an inch and made a deep curtsy. "My lord, my ladyship is in need of . . . um . . . something which I must go belowstairs to get for her. She begs you will pardon her and await her in the drawing room."

It all seemed very suspicious to Ledbetter. He very much feared that his wife was attempting to avoid him, and that she had some intention of backing out of their arrangement to move toward a consummation of their marriage. Therefore he said stiffly, "You may tell your ladyship that I shall await her in the sitting area off my bedchamber, where she can explain her difficulties to me while you are belowstairs."

He heard a gasp from within the room, but ignored it and turned on his heel and stalked across the hall and into his own bedchamber. Really, she was making a great to-do about nothing. Ledbetter paused in front of his mirror to adjust the set of his cravat. He caught a glimpse of his expression in the glass and realized that he looked thoroughly annoyed. Oh, for God's sake! She'd think he was trying to browbeat her. With a great effort he managed to smooth out the fierce lines between his brows and replace them with a look of mild concern.

When he heard footsteps in the hall, he moved swiftly into the sitting area and disposed himself against the mantel. Unfortunately, as it was early, there was no fire lit either in the sitting area or the bedchamber itself, and the room was chilly. His candle provided insufficient light to make the room look welcoming. He would appear the veriest inquisitor.

His bride scratched at the door and let herself in without awaiting his summons. One look at her assured him that she was not of his mother's cast. No suspicion of tears here! Quite the opposite. If Ledbetter had been in the habit of encountering termagants, he might have been more familiar with the martial light in her eyes. As it was, he could tell that she was not happy.

"Really, William, I can think of no reason for you to involve yourself in this matter," she said, glaring at him. "It has *nothing* to do with you. Can I not retire to my room for a space without your hunting me down and demanding an explanation?"

"You were gone for a considerable amount of time. I was concerned that there was some difficulty."

"Well, you needn't be. When I encounter some difficulty which requires your assistance, be assured that I will ask it of you."

The chance that his mother would ever have made such a speech was so remote as to have been an impossibility. Ledbetter very much feared that he had chosen perhaps a little too far in the opposite direction to his mother's meekness. He was not in the habit of having anyone question his actions or speak to him in such a fashion.

"If you would be so good as to explain your difficulty, it would put my mind at ease," he informed her.

Prudence threw her hands up in exasperation. "Ease your mind! Well, there is certainly nothing I wish more than to ease your mind in this instance, William. My difficulty," she said, flushing hotly, "is that I need clean rags."

"I beg your pardon?" He regarded her in some perplexity. "Why in God's name do you need clean rags? And at this hour of the night?"

"Because," she said between clenched teeth, "I have gotten my courses. My monthly cycle, William. Were I at home, I would know precisely where to obtain such items as I need. But I find myself in an unfamiliar house, without the resources I am accustomed to. Does that explain everything to your satisfaction?"

The baron had the grace to flush in his turn. "I beg your pardon! I had no idea!"

"And why should you? But, my dear sir, am I to understand that I shall not be allowed the privacy to deal with this or any other matter I choose to deal with privately?"

"Of course not. I had no intention of invading your privacy, ma'am."

"Nevertheless, you have." Prudence dropped down onto the damask-covered chair opposite to the fireplace and sighed. "Oh, William, I know you're disappointed about my . . . my shyness and my fears. And I truly intend to overcome them. But it is only a few days since we married and I fear I have already tried your patience too far."

"Not at all." Ledbetter moved quickly to stand beside her. He dropped one hand on her shoulder and used the other to lift her face to look at him. "I was very much at fault to seek you out as I did, and to force you to tell me the nature of your distress. I can't promise that I won't do something equally odious another time, Prudence, but I shall certainly try not to."

"Thank you."

"I realize I've forced you to be very frank with me, and you probably don't much care for that." He looked rueful. "But do you know, Prudence, I find it easier to handle than trying to guess what is on your mind."

"Nonsense. You were absolutely appalled when I launched into my diatribe."

"True," he admitted. "But look at the results of your outburst. You told me exactly how you felt, something you would not have done if you'd been trying to be polite and accommodating."

"It's very difficult to be polite and accommodating with you sometimes, William."

"So I gather." He helped her to her feet and gave her a light push in the direction of the door. "I would appreciate your joining me in the Gold Drawing Room when you've taken care of . . . matters."

She dropped a mocking curtsy. "I shan't be overlong, my lord."

"I hope you will take as much time as you need," he retorted.

# Chapter Ten

Prudence joined him in well under half an hour. She found him paging through a leather-bound volume, with several others stacked on a table beside him. At her entry he rose and came toward her, taking her hand and conveying it to his lips.

"My dear," he murmured, a warm light in his eyes.

"My lord," she responded, a little diffidently. "I trust you did not despair of my coming. It was necessary to change my gown."

"I like this one better, in any case," he said. "It is cut considerably lower than the other."

"That is not why I chose it." Though she spoke earnestly, her eyes belied the severity of her words.

"Why did you choose it?"

"Because it is easy to get into."

"Ah, and therefore easy to get out of as well, I trust."

"As you say." Prudence took the chair he indicated, beside his. "Were you looking for something in particular in the books?"

"These?" He waved a hand at the small stack of volumes. "I thought we might read aloud, and I was wondering which would be of the most interest to you. I have a volume of Robert Burns's *Tam o' Shanter,* a work called *Waverly* which I have on good authority is by Walter Scott, or a recent novel by a Lady, called *Emma*."

"Oh, *Emma*, I should think, if it is all the same to you."

"As you wish." Ledbetter returned to his seat and picked up one of the volumes. "I've rung for tea but see no reason why we should not get started. Shall I begin?"

"Please do."

"'*Emma:* A Novel. In three volumes. By the author of "Pride and Prejudice," etc., etc. Vol. 1. 'Emma Woodhouse, handsome, clever, and rich, with a comfortable home and happy disposition, seemed to unite some of the best blessings of existence; and had lived nearly twenty-one years in the world with very little to distress or vex her.' A nice start," he commented, smiling across at his wife.

"Indeed." Prudence disposed herself comfortably on the high-backed armchair and allowed his voice to engross her. He had a rich voice, one to which she could have listened for hours on end. His reading was dramatic and humorous by turns as he detailed life in Highbury and Mr. Woodhouse's objections to Miss Taylor's marriage.

When the tea tray came, he did not pause, but allowed Prudence to pour out and set his cup beside him where he might take a sip as he read. He finished the first chapter of the novel before putting it aside to choose one of the biscuits. "Well, what do you think? We have a whole cast of characters set out so far. I'm especially taken with this Knightley fellow."

Prudence grinned at him. "Perhaps you feel some kinship with him, William. The author says he is the only one who can see faults in Emma."

"Now what could you possibly mean by that?" he wondered. "I am not given to seeing faults in anyone."

"Thank heaven." She set down her cup and asked, "Shall I read for a while?"

"Would you?" Ledbetter handed her the volume and indicated where he had stopped.

Prudence loved reading aloud. It had been a favorite occupation with her and her sisters of a cold, blustery evening at home. She enjoyed the opportunity to take on different voices and accents, to dramatize a bit of poetry or a wrenching scene. As always, she became deeply involved in the story and only noticed Ledbetter's keen interest when she finished a chapter and glanced up.

"What is it?" she asked.

He shook his head. "Nothing. You read charmingly, Prudence. Would you read another chapter?"

"Certainly."

This time she was a little more aware of his gaze upon her but it did not inhibit her enjoyment of the story, or her delight in giving voice to Mr. Woodhouses's absurdities. "A little thin gruel, indeed," she said when she set down the volume at chapter's end. "I daresay you have none of Mr. Woodhouses's eccentricities on that front, William, and will expect your guests to have every type of treat available in March."

"Absolutely." He rose and held a hand out to her. "Come. It's late. We'll read more tomorrow night."

He retained a grip on her hand after she was on her feet and gently tugged her closer to him. She felt a moment of panic when she realized he was going to kiss her, but fought it down.

His mouth on hers was firm. She felt her lips respond to the pressure, as if of their own accord. And then he deepened the kiss, pulled her into the urgency of it somehow. His hands went around her waist, hers lifted to his shoulders to steady herself. The sensations she experienced were unsettling. Little tugs of pleasure occurred here and there in her body. She found that he had pressed her against the long length of him—or she had pressed herself there.

The little tugs of pleasure were becoming more of an

ache, a longing, now. In the most private of places. Prudence felt the warmth of a flush stain her cheeks, and she attempted to draw back. He allowed her to separate from him, but kept a steadying hand on her back.

"Is something the matter?" he asked, a quizzical light in his eyes.

She felt a little breathless. "No. No. But perhaps that should be enough for tonight."

"Oh, I doubt a little more kissing will prove disastrous, my dear. You liked it, did you not?"

"Um . . . yes. But it was beginning to make me nervous."

"Ah . . . nervous." He twined the fingers of one hand with hers, and used them to draw her closer again. "I would not have guessed you to be a woman of nervous disposition."

"I'm not! In the ordinary way I haven't the least tendency toward nerves, I promise you."

"Good. I think it would be most difficult to live with someone of a nervous disposition." He bent his head to kiss her again, allowing his lips to linger on hers for some time. "Does that make you nervous?"

The tugs of urgency had indeed returned. Prudence nodded.

"I see," he said, looking fascinated. He bent his head and began to nibble on her ear. "And that?"

She blinked at him and nodded.

He dropped his lips to the hollow at the base of her neck and kissed that in a most disconcerting way. "That doesn't make you nervous, surely," he suggested.

"But it does." Each time his lips touched her, the same tightening occurred. Her body felt on the edge of a precipice.

"Perhaps it would be better if you kissed me, and I merely stood here."

"I can't see why."

"Well, if my kissing you is making you nervous, then your kissing me should not. I mean, you would be the one actively engaged."

"You're mocking me," she grumbled.

Ledbetter shook his head. "I think you should find out what happens if *you* kiss *me*."

She stood on tiptoe and placed a short firm kiss on his lips. He said patiently, "No, you have to kiss me as though you meant it."

Reluctantly Prudence put her arms around his neck and pulled his head down to hers. Then she tried to duplicate the kind of kiss he had offered her, where she moved her lips on his and exerted pressure to get a response from him. Though she felt certain she was doing it correctly, he made no attempt to meet her pressure with any resistance, or to actively engage her. She realized the frustration he must feel when she didn't respond and she moved a little away from him to meet his gaze.

"You could kiss me, too," she suggested. "I wouldn't mind."

"Yes, but it might make you nervous."

"I would prefer being nervous to feeling ridiculous."

"Then of course I will kiss you back," he agreed.

Prudence once again put her arms around his neck and pressed her lips to his. This time he met her kiss with a tender but delightful response. Prudence found it very exciting to elicit such a direct sensation in answer to her simple touch. If she thought he would take over for her, however, she was mistaken. Ledbetter still awaited her lead. And Prudence rather liked that arrangement.

But the nervousness had definitely returned.

There was a tightness to various locations in her body, which seemed to occur whether it was she doing the kissing, or Ledbetter responding to her. She found herself pressed against his body, her breasts tingling in a most unusual fashion. But even more disconcerting was that aching feeling between her legs which seemed to deepen with the kisses.

Her breathing had quickened, and it was difficult for her to remember what it was she didn't like about the nervousness that kissing brought on. It was unsettling, certainly, but also extremely pleasurable in some ways. She was almost disappointed when Ledbetter drew back and smiled at her.

"Thank you, my dear," he said, carrying her hand to his lips to kiss. "That was very brave of you. I trust you are not overcome by nerves."

"Of course not. I think I could grow accustomed to such a slight indisposition."

"You do?"

"Yes, so long as it goes away afterwards."

He observed her closely. "And has it gone away—this indisposition?"

Prudence could not truthfully say that it had, but it was diminishing. "It's not so strong now. I imagine that in a few minutes I shall be perfectly back to normal."

"No doubt," he said dryly.

"Don't you want me to be back to normal?" she asked, puzzled.

"Well, no. I would prefer that you acclimate yourself to what you call the 'nervousness.' Though you are apparently unaccustomed to it, it is your body's way of preparing for intimate relations between husband and wife."

Prudence flushed a becoming pink. "I don't see how that can be so," she protested. "I should think that would just make it worse."

"But that is because you are thinking that the nervousness is a bad thing. Actually, the changes in your body are a response to stimulation of your desire, and they can be quite pleasurable."

Prudence looked unconvinced. "Perhaps that's true for men, William. I don't think women feel that way."

He shook his head, exasperated. "Prudence, you've told me that you can feel the tension in your body when we kiss. That's what's supposed to happen. Carried to its natural conclusion, that tension is released in a spectacularly pleasant way."

"How?"

"It would be easier to show you than to explain," he said, running a hand through his hair. "Through touching and kissing, that tension builds and builds until it reaches a point where you . . . explode . . . in a most enjoyable fashion."

"Exploding doesn't sound very enjoyable."

"Trust me, it is." He sighed and kissed the tip of her nose. "Are you sure your mother didn't explain all this to you?"

"My mother? Certainly not."

"Your sisters, then. Two more knowledgeable girls I have seldom met."

His wife blushed for her sisters. "They are foolish beyond permission, I grant you. And yes, they have explained to me what husbands and wives do. Why they find it so amusing, I cannot imagine. They terrified me."

"Ah, I see."

"What is it you see, William?"

"That your sisters have given you a distorted view of intimate relations."

Prudence frowned. "I hardly think that is likely." She screwed her courage to the sticking point and asked, "It is true, is it not, that a man breeds with a woman much as animals do?"

Her husband grimaced. "Not precisely, though the equipment in both cases is the same."

"It seems an alarming business, William. In fact, it sounds rather painful to me."

"Sexual congress between men and women is not a painful business, Prudence."

"No?" Prudence fixed him with a steady stare. "Elinor made quite a point of telling me that I would be very much the worse for wear when it happened to me. She insisted that there was a barrier inside a woman which a man had to penetrate, that there was pain and bleeding. I suppose you think that is nothing to distress me."

Ledbetter sighed. "Your sister has overstated the case."

"Now how would you possibly know?" his wife demanded. "Have you been given to deflowering virgins, my lord?"

"Of course not," he all but snapped. "On the other hand, I have never met a woman who even mentioned being hurt the first time she had relations with a man. And it only happens the once!"

"How comforting," Prudence murmured. She paced the sitting room, picking up and replacing various items on the tables—a snuffbox, a book, a candle. Eventually she turned to face him. "You're quite right, of course. It's ridiculous for me to carry on so about such an insignificant matter. Let's get it over with, shall we?"

Ledbetter blinked in astonishment. "I beg your pardon?"

"I'm sure you heard what I said. I shall go up to my room right now and await your arrival. I would ask only that you not dawdle. Just come and take care of the matter."

"Prudence, are you deliberately trying to provoke me?"

"No, how should I be? Or perhaps you would prefer not to do it while I have my monthly cycle. I hadn't thought of that."

"I prefer not to do it at all under such strictures," he muttered. "Attend me, Prudence. I don't want you to consider this some kind of duty, some unbearable obligation. There is a great deal more to it than that."

Ledbetter looked uncomfortable, but he managed to continue nonetheless. "It's like . . . oh, I don't know . . . like waltzing, I suppose. You could be stiff and wooden in someone's arms, or you could be floating, twirling, enjoying the exhilaration of the music and the synchronicity of movement together. For a waltz to be enjoyable, both parties must enter into the spirit of the dance."

He held out a hand to her. "Come, pretend there is music, a gallery of musicians are playing a waltz and you have agreed to stand up with me. The room is filled with spring flowers and the chandeliers are blazing with elegant wax candles."

She hesitated for a long moment and then moved toward him. He clasped her in his arms as on a dance floor, though he held her more closely than he would have in public. His hand felt warm and strong at her waist. He gazed into her eyes and started to hum a familiar waltz. And then they were moving around the floor of the drawing room, skirting furniture as they might have other couples.

At first she felt self-conscious and a little stiff, but he was a remarkably fine dancer and she allowed herself to move with him. He drew her even closer to him, so that their bodies touched. Prudence had never danced quite this way before. She felt the gracefulness of their movements, the excitement of their perfectly attuned turns. She felt one with him.

He danced her into the dark Long Gallery beyond the drawing room, where there was little to hinder their progress. Though she was scarcely familiar with the room, he apparently knew it by heart. She caught glimpses of portraits on the walls as they swung by. He tucked their hands against his cheek and kissed her fingers, even as he guided her expertly about the polished wooden floor. He held her in such a way that she felt fragile and protected and altogether cherished. Dazed, she tried to see his expression in the darkness, but could only detect the gleam of his eyes.

After a very long time, when she was pleasantly dizzy and breathless, he slowed to a stop, but continued to hold her firmly against him. Prudence could feel the beating of his heart. She knew that hers was as rapid from the splendid exercise. She didn't want him to let go of her, and for a long time they remained locked in each other's arms. His breath whispered in her hair and she thought perhaps his lips brushed her temple.

Dancing had never felt like that before. Oh, she had enjoyed the country dances well enough with all their spirited fun, but she had learned to waltz in a formal way that scarcely captured the elegance and intimacy of what they had just accomplished. Her body had felt as lithe and elegant as a bird in flight. And now, pressed against his, it felt lush with possibility.

"Did you enjoy that, Prudence?" he asked softly.

"Very much."

"Do you want me to release you?"

"No."

"Good."

Certainly his lips brushed her forehead now. And then they skimmed over her face, descending to her lips. His kiss was warm and gentle. But for all that, she could feel it tug at her. She returned the pressure and felt her body respond even more strongly.

And his body changed as well. Prudence could feel him harden against her and a flare of panic raced through her, making her shudder slightly. Ledbetter deepened his kiss, allowing her to feel the edge of his desire. But he remained unhurried, his hands lightly stroking her back.

Prudence realized that the sensations in her body were becoming stronger. Her breasts, pressed against his chest, seemed to tingle. The tug at her core felt more like a yearning than like the bout of nerves she'd feared. Ledbetter's hands, rhythmic and soothing on her back, moved slightly lower. They spanned her waist and held her firmly against him. That hard bulge in his pants pressed against her lower abdomen, and instead of being frightened she felt a surprising warmth and need.

His hands moved lower now, slowly tracing the firmness of her buttocks. She had never been touched like this before—and she didn't want him to stop. When his hands cupped her bottom and pressed her lightly against his hardness, she felt a rush of almost giddy urgency. Her pulse beat in her throat. Her hands grasped at his shoulders. She felt his tongue enter her mouth.

She was startled by that. And not certain that she wanted it there. Until he began to explore the recesses of her mouth, to glide his tongue along her own, to move it back and forth in a suggestive way, as though . . . Prudence felt the tension in her body increase once again and she sighed.

Ledbetter continued to hold her tightly against his body but he lifted his head slightly and looked into her eyes. "Does that distress you, Prudence?"

"Mmmm, no."

"Do you mind my holding you so . . . closely?"

"No. Well, it's making my body behave a little strangely."

"But not in a way you dislike," he suggested.

"No, not in a way I dislike," she admitted.

He shifted his hands back to her waist, and then began to move them upward. "Shall I show you something which might give you a great deal of pleasure?"

She hesitated before nodding. His hands continued to move up until they were almost at her breasts. And then, very slowly, very carefully, he traced small circles which got broader and broader. At first they were entirely at her sides, but gradually they moved further onto her breasts. The breath caught in her throat and she could scarcely bear the anticipation. His thumbs rubbed gently across the soft curves as he continued to stare into her eyes.

"Does that feel good, Prudence?" he asked.

She had to swallow before she could answer him. "Yes, very good."

His thumbs had reached the apex of her breasts, and he rubbed them over the place where her nipples were. "Oh," she gasped. "Oh, dear."

She could feel her nipples harden, and her face flush. She was unable to meet his gaze.

"Come, look at me," he urged. "That's what is supposed to happen, my dear. It's a very natural reaction. As is my own."

Prudence knew that he referred to the hard bulge in his pants which she could feel pressing against her groin. She met his eyes and nodded. "I see," she said.

He cupped her breasts in his hands, continuing to stimulate the hardened nipples. "How does that feel?"

"I . . . It feels wonderful."

Ledbetter smiled at her. "Thank God for your honesty, Prudence. I daresay you would prefer not to admit that."

"Yes, for I am still alarmed by the thought of intimate relations."

"An hour ago you urged me to consummate our marriage. I would prefer not to do that until you have a better understanding of the possibilities of pleasure between a husband and wife. And frankly, for one so naive, that won't happen in a day. Shall you mind so very much?" he asked, a teasing note to his voice.

"You are very patient."

"My dear girl, no one has ever accused me of patience before. Let us just say that I am attempting to take the long view of the situation, shall we?"

"Thank you, William. It is very considerate of you."

"No doubt." He gave her one last, brief kiss and released her. "It's late. You must be longing for your bed."

"And do you intend to share my bed tonight?"

"I do." He frowned slightly. "I trust you won't object."

Prudence stood on tiptoe and bravely kissed him. "No, my lord, I won't object."

# Chapter Eleven

Ledbetter was not accustomed to these delays in gratification of his desires. On the other hand, he did not consider himself such a monster as to force himself on his wife simply because they had repeated marriage vows and he could by rights do so. If truth be told, he was a little intrigued by how very naive his wife was. It told him that she had not experienced any of these physical pleasures with her longtime fiancé. Of course, that dunderhead had wandered off to India and remained there, giving absolutely no opportunity for even the most mundane contact with his bride-to-be.

And knowing that his own engagement would last for precisely a week, Ledbetter had not attempted any familiarities with Prudence at her home. But her brazen sisters had led him to the false assumption that his betrothed was a trifle more knowledgeable than she proved to be. No matter. He preferred her innocence.

As the baron prepared for bed, he caught sight of an organ catalog on his bookshelf. How amused his wife had been to hear of the absurd gift his mother had made to the parish. Prudence, it seemed, was destined to surprise him in more ways than he could have anticipated. And while some of those surprises had been initially irritating, more often they were turning out to be enchanting.

Ledbetter stripped off his drawers and wrapped the maroon dressing gown his valet had left out around his body. He didn't bother with the slippers tucked carefully partway under the bed, but walked across the chilly floor to the door as he tied the velvet sash at his waist. Despite the fact that he hadn't given his wife much time to change into her night-clothes, he let himself out into the hall and walked across to knock at her door.

She was still seated at the vanity when he came into the bedroom, but the maid had already left. Prudence had a brush in her hand and she was pulling it through her wild masses of auburn hair. "It's all your fault," she complained ruefully. "When I leave it loose it gets tangled."

"Let me." He took the brush from her fingers and set himself to stroking it through her hair in an easy, unhurried way. "You have the most glorious hair," he told her. "It looked wonderful today. I don't see why you want to pin it down."

"Because then I look like a respectable woman?" she suggested.

"Oh, I don't think anyone would take you for anything but a respectable woman." He set the brush on the vanity and wove his fingers through her hair, all the while watching her in the mirror. "You're the type of woman who could be found alone with the vicar in his bedchamber and people would still not believe the worst of you."

"I'm not sure I find that a flattering encomium, William. I think perhaps you're telling me that I'm a prude and an antidote."

"I trust you know better than that, my dear. Your naiveté has nothing to do with prudishness, and your beauty is self-evident."

Prudence flushed under his steady gaze. "Thank you. I didn't meant to solicit a compliment."

"No, of course you didn't."

He was standing behind her, so that her image blocked almost his entire torso from view in the glass. "Have you ever seen a man naked?" he asked.

Prudence instantly looked alarmed but merely shook her head.

Ledbetter laughed. "And you don't want to. Come, where's your curiosity, ma'am?"

"Where's your modesty?" she asked tartly.

"Ah, there is something you probably don't realize, my dear. Most men haven't a modest bone in their bodies. There's not a one of us who wouldn't quite happily walk around naked all day, given the proper circumstances."

"I find that hard to believe."

"Well, it's true." Ledbetter unfastened the sash at his waist and allowed the dressing gown to fall open, but he was still behind her, so she had no real view of him in the mirror. "Shall I get in bed first?" he suggested.

"If you would."

He laughed, but turned aside and finished removing the dressing gown beside the bed. His wife remained seated at the vanity while he placed the maroon velvet robe over a chair back and climbed into bed. He could not tell if she peeked at him in the mirror or in person, but when he had settled, he patted the bed beside him and said, "Come, it's safe now."

"Safe," his bride muttered, rising from the bench before the mirror. "You don't know the meaning of the word."

She was enveloped in a delightful white cotton confection which covered her from her neck to her toes, but which formed itself rather nicely to her bosom. Prudence did not seem to be particularly aware of this, probably believing that if the gown covered everything right down to her fingertips, it could not possibly be provocative. But it was—to Ledbetter. He groaned.

His bride cocked her head at him and frowned. "What is it? Are you not well, my lord?"

"I'm fine, Prudence. Come to bed."

She snuffed the candle on the vanity and in the darkness he could hear her light tread across the carpet. When she reached the side of the bed, she hesitated and said, "You'll have to move over a little, William."

"Of course, my dear." He shifted, though only a very little distance. She gave a tsk of annoyance, but he held firm. "There's plenty of room for you."

"You obviously have a distorted idea of my size," she said, as she climbed onto the high bed.

"No. I just want to snuggle against you."

"That's not really a good idea," she protested, as she slipped onto the bed and could not avoid pressing her back right up against him.

"Oh, I think it is." He encircled her with his arms, not surprised to find her own arms folded tightly across her chest. "Can you trust me enough to relax?"

For a while there was no response. Then he felt her body lose some of its stiffness, though her arms remained where they were. He wrapped his naked body around her, gently cradling her in his arms. "It's tomorrow that your new maid comes, is it not?" he asked.

"Why, yes. Her father is to bring her in the morning. You're not still angry with me about that, are you?"

"Was I angry? More surprised, I think. And perhaps a bit disconcerted. I had pictured Mrs. Collins finding someone for you. But it scarcely matters, Prudence. I trust she'll work out well."

"I think she will. She seems quite a clever girl, and not easily intimidated."

"Ah. An important attribute, not being intimidated. I'm delighted that you possess it, Prudence."

"You mock me, William."

"Not at all."

"I cannot think it would be very comfortable, having a husband who intimidated one."

"No, I daresay it wouldn't. And yet, do you know, I think my mother was intimidated by my father. At least by his—blustering, was what my friend Geoffrey called it. He would get quite red in the face and yell as though everyone around him was deaf as a post."

"Your poor mother! Did he . . . did he strike out?"

"Good Lord, no. But his roar was enough to make Mama shudder." Ledbetter stroked a thumb along her arm. "I know I suffer from the same kind of impatience, Prudence, and I'm sorry for it. But I try very hard never to raise my voice, and if I should ever do so, you have only to call upon my father's name to remind me of how devastating a habit it can be."

He felt her tremble in his arms. "I'm sorry. Have I frightened you? I meant to do the opposite."

"No," she said in a strangled voice. "You haven't frightened me."

He kissed the back of her head. "Good. I want you to learn to feel comfortable with me."

He felt a sigh, or perhaps it was a sob, wrack her body. "You must think me such a fool, William," she whispered. "So stupidly childish."

"Nonsense." He tightened his arms protectively around her. "Two weeks ago you scarcely knew who I was, Prudence. And now I'm in your bed. I understand that you need some time to adjust. Don't distress yourself about it. Go to sleep. You must be exhausted."

He felt her head nod against his lips, and he kissed her hair again. And wondered where this reserve of patience came from, since he was so unfamiliar with it. But before he could delve deeply into the thought, he had fallen asleep himself.

Prudence was awakened by the careful movements of her husband as he climbed from their bed. She kept her eyes shut tight as he pulled the coverlet up to her neck and placed a soft kiss on her brow. When she felt certain he had turned away from the bed, she opened her eyes just a slit. He was picking up his dressing gown from the chair and she had a full view of his back side.

He looked almost larger naked than he did in his clothes. From this angle she could see that his shoulders were broad, his waist narrow and his legs strong. As he slipped into the dressing gown, his body turned and she found herself observing his male parts. She swallowed hard as she remembered that once in the night his member had hardened against her and she'd heard him mutter a plaintive oath. He had rolled away from her, then, and she'd fallen back to sleep. But later she had found herself once again in his arms.

She closed her eyes again and feigned sleep as her husband left the room. Ledbetter was not completely correct in his statement that she had scarcely known him until two weeks ago. She remembered him, as he had apparently remembered her, from her coming-out Season. Else why would he have come to her recently? True, she had inherited a deal of money, and for some reason he seemed to need to have that money at his disposal, but if he had been a complete stranger, he would not have shown up at her home, even under the auspices of her neighbors, the Rightons.

No, Ledbetter had noticed her when she had her Season. And she had noticed him. But his intensity had frightened her. There was something so overpoweringly male about him, so fraught with an undercurrent of desire, that she had trembled at his touch even when they danced a country

dance. Never before tonight had she waltzed with him—
which seemed now a very good thing. For look at the effect
he had had on her. Lord, she would have swooned on the
dance floor as a girl of eighteen!

Ledbetter safe? Hardly. It was Allen who had been safe.
So gentle and kind to her, so patient and understanding of
her physical shyness. A gentleman through and through.
Never the least sign of urgency in his touch. He had only
kissed her a few times, and they hadn't been at all like the
kisses Ledbetter bestowed on her. What had possessed her to
marry him? He was far too physical a man for her to cope
with.

Prudence sighed as she pushed back the coverlet and
climbed out of bed. She would have to overcome her distress. Ledbetter was showing an astonishing consideration
of her difficulties, but she could not expect his patience to
last forever. She grimaced at herself in the mirror and pulled
the bell cord for the maid.

Tessie arrived midmorning and was brought by Mrs.
Collins to the small withdrawing room Prudence had appro-
priated on the ground floor. There was a fine Sheraton desk
in the room where she had taken to organizing her thoughts
and penning her lists and letters. Tessie's eyes were
sparkling with excitement, and her cheeks glowed from the
brisk drive to Salston. She dropped a respectful curtsy to
Prudence and hastened to say, "I hope I am not too early,
Lady Ledbetter, but I made Papa start at dawn!"

Her new mistress laughed. "So eager as that to start your
duties. Well, you have met Mrs. Collins, who is our housekeeper. She will show you, as she is showing me, how to go
on here."

"She was that nice to me, ma'am. Said as how they all
welcomed me and hoped I would be happy here."

"I, too, hope you shall. But if you are not, don't keep it a secret. If you will speak to me about any difficulties, I will do my best to see that they are sorted out."

Prudence sat back in her chair and studied the young woman. "Do you know how to read and write, Tessie?"

"Oh, yes, my lady. Our folks taught each of us, saying if we didn't know, them as did would take advantage. Begging your pardon."

"Well, they were probably quite right." Prudence indicated a list she'd been preparing on the desk. "My husband has desired me to arrange for a dinner party for the neighbors in a week's time, and I would find it immensely helpful if you would serve as my assistant. Frankly, I don't think your duties as my dresser will be particularly onerous, especially as Ledbetter is determined that I shall leave my hair quite untamed."

"Fancy a gentleman seeing how remarkable your hair is!" the girl exclaimed, surprised. "In my experience men don't notice such things at all. A poor girl is fortunate if a fellow remembers what *color* her hair is."

"I should deem myself fortunate indeed, then," Prudence said dryly. "Would you be willing to assist me with the arrangements for the party?"

"Oh, yes. What is it you'd like me to do?"

Prudence gazed absently out the window, drumming her fingers on the desk. "I should like to do something a little special, but not so different as to alarm our neighbors. Let me think about it for a while. But in the meantime, you might help me address the invitations if you've a good hand." Prudence looked at her questioningly.

"Fair enough, I think." Tessie pointed to a sheet of foolscap on the desk and asked, "May I?"

"Certainly." Prudence watched as the girl dipped a quill in the standish and wrote her own name with a flourish on the

sheet of paper. "Very nice, Tessie. I'll request a list from
Ledbetter, or better yet from Mrs. Collins, and we'll make
an afternoon of it, shall we?"

"Oh, yes, my lady. I'll just put my valise up in the room
I'm to share with Betsy, while you get the list. If that is satisfactory?"

When the girl had gone, Prudence continued to stare out
the window for some time. It would be weeks before spring
brought a profusion of blossoms to the countryside around
Salston. The landscape looked winter-dreary and barren. But
Prudence could picture it in a month's time, with grass
growing green again and trees budding and daffodils poking
their heads up above the ground to brighten the flower beds.

She wouldn't be the only one weary of winter, she realized, and a plan began to take shape in her mind. She rang
for Mrs. Collins, and when the housekeeper came, Prudence
asked, "Salston has succession houses, I believe, Mrs.
Collins?"

"Two, milady. One for fruits and vegetables, and the other
for flowering plants. The baron's mama was fond of her
roses and her stocks. And the gardener has a wonderful way
with the spring bulbs—daffodils, narcissi, hyacinths, tulips.
It won't be long before he'll have some blooms to bring in
for us."

"How lovely. Well, I should like to speak to him, Mrs.
Collins. Ledbetter has asked that I give a dinner party for
our neighbors next week and having spring blooms around
for it would be very welcome." She gestured to the chair beside her desk and said, "Please, sit down, if you will. I
should like you to give me an idea of whom Ledbetter will
expect, and on what scale he is accustomed to entertaining."

Mrs. Collins was a reservoir of information. As she listed
the young and old of the neighborhood whom Ledbetter
might be expected to invite she filled Prudence in on where

people lived in relationship to Salston, how long they had been in the neighborhood, how close was the association between their families and Ledbetter's, and a host of other useful details. Prudence busily scratched a list of names as the housekeeper talked, adding notes in the margins that might be helpful in remembering just who each person was.

"Thank you!" she exclaimed when Mrs. Collins at length decided she had covered everyone possible. "And the menu? Will Ledbetter wish to have a hand in that?"

"Oh, I shouldn't think so, Lady Ledbetter. His lordship was never one to involve himself. Best you discuss it with cook."

"Only if you will guide me," Prudence insisted. "At this time of year at Colwyck we would have guinea fowls and a forequarter of lamb, along with braised capon and ducklings for such a dinner. But I'm unfamiliar with the availability and desirability of such items here at Salston. Have you a source of red mullet and fillets of whiting?"

"His lordship isn't fond of mullet, but for this large a party I'm sure he'd wish to offer it. He's that fond of a spring soup removed by boiled turbot and lobster sauce. And we usually have a rump of beef *à la jardiniere*, a garnished boiled tongue, and larded sweetbreads. And a ham."

Prudence quickly scribbled down the dishes as Mrs. Collins rattled them off. Obviously no one went away hungry after dining at Salston, she thought ruefully. When Mrs. Collins had agreed to send Cook to her, Prudence sat back in her chair and frowned again at the winter landscape. Not just a few vases of flowers on the table and sideboard, she decided, but something more exciting and unique. If the gardener was able to handle it, of course.

And she'd only find that out if she visited him on his own turf.

# Chapter Twelve

So just before luncheon, Prudence wrapped a warm shawl about her and went in search of Mr. Newhall. He was not difficult to find, as he spent a fair amount of the winter months in the succession houses and the toolshed, preparing for spring. He was an incredibly old man, with a balding head and arthritic fingers. But he seemed spry enough as he darted among the benches, checking this plant and then that one, plucking off a dead leaf and propping up a drooping branch.

Prudence observed him through the glass for a few minutes before pulling open the metal and glass door and letting herself into the first of the succession houses. Though she made a fair amount of noise, stomping to knock the dirt off her shoes, Mr. Newhall didn't turn around. Odd, she thought, and called to him. But he continued to work with the plant before him, obviously unaware of her presence.

Why, he's deaf, Prudence realized. Oh, Lord, how will I talk to him? And why didn't someone mention his deafness?

As she moved toward him, Mr. Newhall must have caught a glimpse of movement from the corner of his eye, because he turned to face her. "Why, it's the new Lady Ledbetter," he said quite clearly, and rather loudly. "Welcome to Salston, my lady. I'm Newhall."

"How do you do, Mr. Newhall? I hope you won't mind my coming unannounced."

He appeared to watch her lips. Could he understand her?

"Glad to have you, my lady," he boomed. "Let me show you around."

Oh, yes, the flowers were already beginning to bloom. In a week . . . Prudence felt a thrill of anticipation. In addition to the narcissi and daffodils, there was blue scilla and grape-colored muscari. The crocus came in gold and purple and white. The air was lively with the sweet scent of hyacinth and the musky odor of the muscari.

"How wonderful!" she breathed. "Mr. Newhall, next week we are giving a dinner party for the neighbors. I should like to have spring flowers for it, but not just in vases. I would like to turn the dining room into a garden."

He looked puzzled and tilted his head questioningly. "Eh? You want flowers for a dinner party?"

"Yes, but not cut." She made a snipping gesture with her fingers and shook her head. "Like this." She made a sweeping motion with her hands that took in the whole of the benches with their planter boxes full of spring flowers. "Instead of moving these outside to the garden beds, I would like them inside—in the dining room. Do you understand what I mean?"

"I don't hear so well," he explained, "but I can tell by your lips some of what you're saying. You want me to bring the planter boxes in the house?"

He sounded so incredulous that Prudence laughed. "Yes," she admitted. "Inside. Like a garden, or at least like a border around the room. Would it be possible?"

"Never done something like that," he said, frowning. "Take a bit of work, and I'd need two, three helpers."

"I would see that you got all the assistance you needed," Prudence promised.

"Big room, is it?" he asked.

"Enormous."

"I'll need to take a gander at it, my lady. Sooner is better."

"Right now, if you wish."

"You ask his lordship about this?"

"Not yet."

He grinned suddenly and nodded. "Daresay I can manage, with help. Let's take a look."

Prudence was not certain that Mr. Newhall understood exactly what she wanted, owing to his deafness. And yet, as he prowled the dining room, past the sideboards on each side, and around the mahogany table with its impressive collection of matching mahogany chairs, he began to talk out loud. "Two rows of planters where there's no furniture, and one where there is. Mind, the footmen won't like it one bit! You'll have to speak to them. Can't have those big feet stepping in the dirt and the tulips! Train them ahead of time, see?"

He looked directly at her and she nodded.

"Won't take less than thirty planters, I'm thinking. Don't know as I have that many in the succession house. I could force a few of the later blooms—the wallflower, the lily of the valley."

"Or," Prudence suggested almost hesitantly, "you could make the back planter a rock garden of sorts, with rock phlox and rock campanula and rock rose climbing over and around the rocks in a kind of carpet."

His old eyes twinkled at her. "That I could, my lady. Mayhap t'would be even better than just rows of those showy bulbs. You done this before?"

"No. The idea just came to me this morning. You don't think Ledbetter would object, do you?"

"Can't see why. His mama was that fond of flowers, don't you know. I should think he'd be right pleased." He cocked his head at her. "Why don't you ask him?"

"Well, I thought I might make it a surprise." She regarded

him with a doubtful frown. "Unless you thought that wouldn't be wise."

"Can't see the harm in it. Nothing to fly in the boughs over, leastways. But that's for you to decide."

"Yes. And the floors, Mr. Newhall? How would we best protect them?"

He stroked his chin as he contemplated the dark stained wood for several minutes. "There's a roll of old nursery carpet in the stable attic. Saw it myself not six months past. No use to anyone. We'll cut it up to put under the planters. If we bring them in that day, we won't need to water them here, so the floors'll be safe enough."

"Oh, perfect. I'm afraid it will be a great deal of work."

"For a great reward, if I do say so, ma'am. Something out of the ordinary. The baron will be proud."

"Do you think so?" That was precisely what Prudence hoped. "Oh, thank you, Mr. Newhall. You're kind to indulge my whimsy. Be sure to get all the help you need, and let me know if there is anything I should do to make it work."

"That I will, my lady."

When he had gone, Prudence looked around the room, envisioning the garden that would appear there. She hoped it would seem magical rather than pretentious to Ledbetter's neighbors. But they were country people, as she was, and they must be as tired of winter as she was. Surely an early spring display would be just the thing to perk up spirits and encourage the warmth and hopefulness of that delicious season.

When Ledbetter joined her for their midday meal, he noticed a suppressed air of excitement about her. "Dare I ask what has you in a state of high excitement, my dear?" he queried as he helped himself to a pork cutlet.

"Oh, it is merely my planning for the dinner next week,"

she said, waving a hand in dismissal. "Mr. Newhall has such a fine display of early spring flowers. Ledbetter, how long has he been deaf?"

His gaze rose swiftly to hers and he frowned. "Deaf? Newhall? I am not aware of it."

"He is quite capable of telling what you're saying when you face him. Either he understands the movement of one's lips, or his hearing is not entirely gone. But when I approached him from behind, he was completely unaware of me."

"You must be mistaken, Prudence. Someone would have mentioned it if he were deaf."

"Not necessarily. He's an old man and your staff might have been afraid you would retire him if you knew. I trust you will not."

"Perhaps he *should* be retired."

"I shall regret that I told you if you're going to take such a stand. He's obviously a genius with plants and it would probably break his heart to be retired from Salston."

"For God's sake, Prudence, you can't know that! He may long for a chance to spend his days in a rocking chair out in the sun, without having to lift a finger in anyone's garden for the rest of his days."

She glowered at him. "And he may prefer to work in the succession houses and out in the gardens. I should think he would be particularly offended to be pensioned off just because he's lost his hearing. And don't you dare do a thing about it before the dinner party next week, for I depend upon him to provide me with spring blooms for the house."

"I'm sure Newhall is not the only one who can provide spring blooms."

"It is all arranged, William, and I would be most distressed if you were to put all my plans in disarray. Promise me that you will not."

His natural impatience was rising. The management of Salston, after all, was his obligation, not hers. And if he had an employee who had become deaf and deserved to be generously pensioned off, he wanted no interference in his ability to act as he chose.

"I shall have to deal with the matter as I see fit," he insisted, intending to put a period to the discussion.

"Am I to understand that you take no account of my wishes, William?" his wife asked in a surprisingly chilly voice.

"You have nothing to say to this matter. It is entirely my province."

"But I *have* said something. I have said that I would be most distressed if you were to put all my plans in disarray."

"I can hardly put your plans in disarray by pensioning off old Newhall," he protested, annoyed. "Really, it has nothing to do with you."

To his astonishment, his wife rose from the table and excused herself. Before he had settled on what exactly to say to her, she had left the room. Dumbfounded, Ledbetter stared after her.

Prudence had never done anything comparable to walking out on her husband at luncheon. On the one hand she felt indescribably guilty for behaving so badly. On the other she was so seriously annoyed that she could scarcely bring herself to sit still. At first she went to her room and attempted to read, but, afraid that Ledbetter would show up there and berate her (with his voice unraised, of course), she quickly decided to leave the house.

Escaping by way of the side door, she wrapped the ragged shawl he'd provided previously around her shoulders to ward off the cold breeze that blew around the corner of the building. The wind played havoc with her unrestrained hair and nipped at her ears, but she continued to stalk off across the yard toward the home wood. Nothing was likely to cool her temper so effectively as freezing to death, she decided grimly.

This kind of scene would never have taken place if she'd married Allen. For one thing, Allen would have been all consideration of her. And for another, he would have paid attention to her simplest request. Oh, why had she even mentioned Newhall's deafness to Ledbetter? She should have known that he would behave perversely.

And how was she to manage living with a man like that? Though Prudence had always considered herself to have a reasonably mild disposition, she was finding that it was far from difficult for Ledbetter to set up her back. It almost felt as though he did it on purpose.

Within the shelter of a stand of alder Prudence paused to catch her breath. She could hear the starlings cry above and watched as a mistle-thrush flew with twigs to build a nest. There was the murmur of a stream nearby. She followed an overgrown path in the direction of the sound and came in time to a meandering creek that rolled over mossy rocks and lapped at its muddy banks.

The peacefulness of the scene calmed her. With a shaky sigh Prudence dropped down onto a rotting log and allowed herself to absorb the gentle sounds of nature all around her. She would have to apologize to Ledbetter, of course, and she disliked apologizing. Especially when she was still convinced that he was entirely in the wrong.

Prudence sat for some time with her elbows on her knees, her chin on her locked fingers. Her tumultuous emotions gradually dwindled to a vague discontent. Well, what had she expected, agreeing to marry Ledbetter on such short reacquaintance, and with the full knowledge that it was her money he needed? Though why, when she looked at the per-

fectly groomed estate around her he should be in the least
need of ready cash, she could hardly imagine.

Some gambling debt, perhaps. Gentlemen were so ludicrous about their play-and-pay rules. They could merrily
leave their tailors and bootmakers to starve, but heaven for-
bid they should delay the payment of a gambling loss to one
of their rich friends.

A brown hare bounded alongside the stream, pausing momentarily to dip its mouth in the water. Prudence watched as
it hopped back into the woods. Her gaze, lifted from the
stream, now came to rest on her husband, who was leaning
against a tree across the water, staring at her. She could feel
a flush rise to her cheeks, but she refused to budge from the
log. Let him come to her if he chose, or go away again and
leave her alone.

When it became obvious that she intended to remain
where she was, he gave an exaggerated sigh and headed toward her. He easily cleared the stream in one leap and seated
himself beside her on the log. "You'll ruin your gown," he
pointed out.

"Then I'll buy another one," she retorted. "With that generous allowance you've granted me."

His brows rose in surprise. "Isn't it? I agreed to precisely
what your father requested."

"It's far too much," she complained bitterly. "No woman
consigned to country life could possibly go through the half
of it."

"Am I to understand that you would prefer a smaller allowance," he asked carefully, "or that you would prefer to
spend time in London?"

"I'm sure my wishes are not of the least concern to you."

"Ah, of course not. I'd forgotten."

Prudence, who had been avoiding his eyes, now attempted to meet them. "I'm sorry I behaved so inexcusably, William. It was childish of me to walk out on you."

"Yes, it was. I trust you won't feel the need to do it again."

"I should think that will depend entirely upon you," she said, smiling sweetly.

"My dear lady, you can't hold *me* responsible for *your* behavior."

"Whyever not? You hold everyone else responsible for making you impatient, do you not?"

"How did this get to be about me?"

"I believe it was you who insisted upon ignoring my very plainly expressed and entirely reasonable request."

"So it was. How could I have forgotten that?"

"And I should like to know how you found me here in the woods, too. I came here to be alone."

"I saw you from the dining room window, scurrying across the lawn in that ridiculous shawl, and was afraid you would freeze to death."

"I was not scurrying," she retorted. "And I would remind you that this is the very same shawl you offered me for our drive to the Mannings."

"How could I forget?" Ledbetter eyed her wildly disordered hair and her pink nose. "You must be devilishly cold, Prudence. Won't you come in with me?"

"Am I forgiven?"

Ledbetter grunted and ran a hand through his own windblown hair. "If I am," he said, somewhat grudgingly.

Prudence nodded. "It was just that I had planned something special, a surprise for you, with Newhall, William. Something I thought you would be pleased with. And if he is not here to bring it about . . ." She lifted her shoulders in a helpless shrug. "I never meant to interfere or question your authority."

"You're going to be the ruin of me," he muttered. "Every

time I get impatient with you, it turns out I'm an ass to have done so. I foresee a time, which will come very shortly, when I'm too intimidated by the possibility of once again proving myself a numbskull to indulge my worst habit. Then where shall I be? A perfectly reasonable human being."

Prudence giggled. "You're absurd. And," she added, dropping her eyes, "you have been exceedingly patient with me . . . in certain things."

"So I have!" he agreed in a mocking voice. "I have proven that I am not entirely a brute, have I not?"

"You have." Prudence rose and dusted off the wood chips from her skirts. Ledbetter adjusted the shawl around her shoulders and then allowed his fingers to stray through her hair. She looked up at him with a puzzled frown.

"I love your hair," he said.

"It is very odd of you."

He laughed and placed a kiss on her cold nose. "Not at all. Has no one told you before how glorious it is?"

"No. Though Tessie seems to admire it as well. I can't think why."

Ledbetter merely shook his head and tucked her arm through his. "Let's get you back to a warm fire. And you're probably hungry. We'll have an early tea."

# Chapter Thirteen

The baron was finding that being married was entirely different from what he had supposed it would be. What he had said to his bride about his discomposure was entirely true. It was a new experience for him to be held accountable for his behavior in just such a way. Not that he was accustomed to riding roughshod over his employees and acquaintance. But it had not actually occurred to him that he might in fact misjudge the simplest situation and then be shamed into apologizing for his actions or words.

And he wouldn't have believed it possible if he *had* considered the matter, either.

Yet here was a chit of a girl insisting that he behave like a gentleman. Imagine! Ledbetter smiled ruefully as he observed himself in the mirror while he dressed for dinner. He had seldom been as startled in his life as when Prudence had walked out of their midday meal. On the other hand, he had been genuinely touched to hear that she was planning a surprise for him. How could he comfortably reconcile the two facets of her character? And did he need to?

The truth was that she charmed him. Those big, honest eyes. That sensational hair. Her warmth and humor. Her delight with even the smallest things. Her response to his kiss and his touch. Oh, she was worth learning a little patience for. And he had every intention of convincing her that she had not made a mistake in marrying him.

Ledbetter, lost in thought, allowed his valet to accomplish a rather complicated and distinguished neckcloth arrangement without shifting in irritation. His man regarded him speculatively, but said nothing as he carefully brushed down Ledbetter's jacket and tweaked it until it fit perfectly over his broad shoulders. When the man reached up to give one more finicky touch to the cravat, however, the baron grimaced.

"It will be fine, Balliot," he said. "Thank you."

"Very good, my lord."

"Don't wait up for me," Ledbetter added, as he had each night since he had arrived at Salston. Though he knew it pained Balliot to find the baron's clothes carelessly tossed on the bed, Ledbetter did not lead his life to please his servants. "I'll ring for you when I need you in the morning."

"Very good, sir."

Ledbetter waited until the valet had departed before crossing the hall to knock on his wife's door. Tessie answered immediately and dropped a hasty curtsy. "Lady Ledbetter is almost ready, Lord Ledbetter," she said.

"Welcome to Salston, Tessie," he said, observing the girl carefully as she rose from her curtsy. There was nothing submissive about her posture, though there was nothing insolent, either. On the whole he thought perhaps he preferred that self-confident air to the one of obsequiousness with which he was more frequently faced.

"Thank you, sir. It's a lovely house, and the people have been ever so kind."

"I'm pleased to hear it." His gaze shifted to his wife, who stood before the mirror with a different earring in each hand. She wore a gown of burgundy zephryine and looked particularly fetching. "May I come in, Prudence?"

"Certainly. We were just debating the wisdom of garnets

with the burgundy gown or pearls. You may decide if you wish."

"The garnets," he said instantly. Then he lifted a hand and said, "No, wait. I have something of my mother's that would suit you and that gown admirably."

He had meant to save them for the night of their party, but the present seemed as good a time as any to bestow them on his bride. It took him but a moment to retrieve them from the strongbox in his sitting room, but when he returned he found that Tessie had gone and Prudence was alone. He smiled his approval.

"It wasn't my idea," Prudence admitted. "Tessie said she would be in the way if you were going to present me with some family heirloom. I assured her it was no such thing, but she insisted."

"Obviously she's as clever as you assumed, my dear, for I do indeed intend to bestow a family heirloom on you."

His wife flushed. "There's no need, really, William. The garnets will look quite attractive with my dress."

"These will look better," he insisted.

The old jewelry case had been through several generations, but its contents sparkled as brightly as the day they were cut. The diamond necklace and earring set gleamed in the candlelight against its plush velvet bed. Prudence took a step backward, her eyes flying to Ledbetter's. "But they must be worth a fortune!" she exclaimed.

"I daresay they are. Been in the family for nearly a century."

"But, William, they should go to your sister!"

"No, these are for my wife. They have always been for the Baroness Ledbetter. One of the advantages of the job," he teased. "Don't you like them, Prudence?"

"They're the most beautiful jewels I've ever seen."

Gratified, he lifted the necklace from the case and put it

around her neck. The clasp was an awkward one, and it took him a moment to get the hang of it. By the time he was able to observe the sparkling stones against her chest, he found his wife staring at herself in the mirror, bemused.

"But, William, just for dinner, the two of us. They should be saved for special occasions."

"Well, I had intended to give them to you next week when we have the neighbors in, but I can see no reason the neighbors should enjoy them before I do. They look lovely on you, my dear. Here. Try the earrings."

When she stood before him in the matching set of diamonds, Ledbetter felt an unfamiliar tightness in his chest. This was the woman with whom he was destined to spend his life. She looked magnificent, every inch a baroness. How had he managed to choose a woman so perfectly suited to be mistress of Salston?

Prudence interrupted his train of thought, the bemused smile still on her face. "Thank you, William. They're magnificent."

"They become you." He frowned a little as he studied her face. "You know, I believe there is a matching tiara somewhere. I'll look it out before next week."

"I hardly think the occasion will be grand enough for me to wear a tiara," she said with amusement. "One day, if you take me to a ball, I shall be delighted to wear it."

"*If* I take you to a ball? My dear girl, I'm sure there will be numerous occasions on which we attend balls together."

He was surprised to see the doubt in her eyes, but she merely smiled and said, "Of course. Though no one will be able to see a tiara if you insist on my leaving my hair wild this way."

"Your hair is like some exotic bird's plumage. It declares your uniqueness. You should be proud of it, Prudence."

She flushed slightly and dipped her head in acknowledgement of his compliment. "Shall we go down now?"

"Certainly, if you're ready." Ledbetter resisted a strong impulse to kiss his bride and instead moved to hold her bedroom door open. Very much to his surprise, she paused when she came abreast of him and stood on tiptoe to place a shy, sweet kiss on his lips. Then she immediately continued through the door and out into the hall.

Prudence felt as though the diamonds bestowed an unusual animation on her. Throughout dinner she fancied that she sparkled as richly as the stones did in the light from the chandelier. She told amusing stories about the village where she had lived all her life, and discussed with intelligence the writers whose books Allen had sent her to read. And she drew Ledbetter out about his interests in archeology and Greek myths.

For hours they sat across the enormous table from each other, talking and laughing as though they were the best of friends and the most equal of minds. It was the most stimulating evening Prudence could remember ever experiencing. And when they at length adjourned to the drawing room, Ledbetter seated himself close beside her on the sofa and read to her from *Emma* in that deep, lovely voice of his.

She liked the solid feel of his arm and thigh against hers. His left hand held the volume with ease while he prepared to turn a page with the fingers of his right. Prudence found herself watching his hands, and remembering where he had placed them on her body the previous evening. And the sensations that they had elicited from her. She wondered if he would do that again—touch her that way. To her surprise, the thought, though a little alarming, was more one of anticipation than dread.

After a while she found it difficult to keep her mind on the story, for thinking about what might happen when Ledbetter set down the leather-bound book and turned to her. But he continued to read, obviously unaware of her curiosity, and Prudence eventually found it necessary to simulate a cough to draw his attention.

"Shall I ring for tea?" he asked, concerned. "Perhaps you need something to soothe your throat."

"No, no, it's nothing. In fact I'd be happy to read for a while. You must be ready for a break."

"If you're sure . . ."

Prudence took the book from him, thinking that she would be able to concentrate better if she were the one reading. And, perhaps, thinking that with his hands free he might find a better use for them than turning pages. But Ledbetter used his hands to pull the bell cord, ordering tea when the footman appeared in response. Well, nothing was going to happen with servants about to descend upon them, Prudence thought, and attempted to focus her whole attention on the developing situation in the novel.

It was when she had finally managed to shift her thoughts that Ledbetter's hands slid around her waist. He did no more than stroke her side with his thumb, but it was enough to remind her of the previous evening. She stole a glance at him, only to find that he was sitting with his eyes closed, intent on her voice. There was a tap on the door before a footman brought in the tea tray, but Ledbetter did not hastily (or even leisurely) remove his hand from where it rested.

Prudence thanked the footman and, when he had departed, poured tea for the two of them. Ledbetter withdrew his hand from her waist with a sigh and accepted his cup of tea.

Prudence was not displeased when her husband followed her into her bedroom and waited while she dismissed the waiting Tessie. Her new maid looked not the least surprised by this development, but dropped a graceful curtsy and wished her mistress good night. When the door had closed behind her, Prudence turned hesitantly to him.

"Come here," he said, holding his arms open to her.

Prudence moved a little stiffly into them and he drew her against his body. For a very long time he merely held her there, stroking her back and whispering encouragement into her ear. "Let me show you pleasure, my sweet. Let me touch you until you experience your body's need and its fulfillment. Just that. Just for you tonight. I promise."

"It's not fair to you," she whispered.

"There's plenty of time for me," he assured her. "May I take off your gown?"

She nodded and moved back from him. His fingers were so sure on the buttons that Prudence couldn't help but wonder how many women he had undressed in his past. And would there be others in the future? Soon he lifted the gown over her head and left her standing in the middle of the room in her shift and the magnificent diamonds.

"You should take the jewelry off first," she suggested.

But he smiled at her and shook his head. "I have the greatest desire to see you naked in the diamonds, Prudence. Well, perhaps not entirely naked, this time." He turned her toward the mirror and stood behind her. His hands came to rest at her sides, very, very close to her breasts. And he stroked her there, where she could watch what he was doing in the glass. His fingers moved slowly but steadily onto the mounds of her breasts, and Prudence found that she was holding her breath.

An excitement leaped through her body, making her breasts feel aching and her lower abdomen tight. Ledbetter's hands had begun to massage the fullness of her bosom, causing her an exquisite sensation. Her face became flushed and her eyes sought his in the mirror. "I don't understand what's happening," she whispered.

"Your body is becoming aroused. Touching your breasts is part of making love, Prudence. The sensations you feel are preparing your body for intercourse."

His fingers had reached the peak of her breasts and through the cotton of the shift she could feel that her nipples were firm. As he rubbed the taut peaks, a deeper sensation swirled through her body and she heard herself moan. She saw him smile in the mirror before he turned her back toward him. With one hand he pushed the fabric down to expose one of her breasts and Prudence shuddered.

"It's all right," he said softly. "There is something I can do which will make your breast feel even more wonderful, if you will allow me."

Prudence could feel the pulse beating in her throat. Perhaps this was enough for one evening. Perhaps it would be better if she called a halt to this game they were playing. "Yes," she said, because his touch was making her weak with a feverish kind of need.

But she had not expected what happened next. He lowered his head and took the tip of her breast in his mouth! "Oh, I don't think . . ." And then the sensation of his suckling on her spun through her body and she felt her knees buckle. Ledbetter's arm came around her to support her, but his mouth did not release her nipple. It drew on her—deeply, hungrily. The swirl of sensations filled Prudence, making her ache with a need she hadn't known existed. "Oh, God."

Ledbetter nudged the fabric down over the other breast and took that neglected nipple into his mouth. Prudence thought she would die from the exquisite agony of his mouth and tongue on her. How could she not have known such feelings existed?

Her husband released her breast after a long moment and

stepped back to look at her. "God, you're beautiful," he sighed, bringing a hand up to cup each breast. "How are you feeling now, Prudence?"

"Amazed," she admitted. "It's like nothing I've ever felt. I don't want you to stop."

"I hope not." Ledbetter dropped his head to her breast again and drew the nipple in, teasing it with his lips, tasting it with his tongue, until her breath quickened and she put her hands around him for support.

Ledbetter shifted her into his arms and carried her to the bed, where he sat down with her in his lap. She could feel his hardness beneath her, and it made her a little nervous. But he distracted her with kisses and the incredible touch of his hands on her breasts. She could feel the need rising in her like yeast, swelling her flesh, making her feel ripe and on the edge of a luscious precipice.

And then he stopped. He drew back from her to study her face and her dazed eyes. "I'm going to take my clothes off now," he announced.

Prudence flushed but made an effort to help by loosening the knot of his cravat and tugging it off. Ledbetter shifted so that she could assist him out of his coat as well. She rose from his lap to hang the coat over the back of the chair, and fold the white linen cravat carefully on the seat. In the meantime Ledbetter had removed his shirt and was in the process of stripping down his pants and drawers together when Prudence turned back.

"Oh, dear," she murmured, seeing for the first time his male member in such a state. She turned her head away, her hands fluttering helplessly.

He rose to stand behind her, gently taking her into his arms, but not turning her around. "That delicious state of arousal that you've been feeling, Prudence, well, in a man, it's even more evident. That's all it means, that I'm aroused. I've promised you that I won't enter you tonight, haven't I?"

"Yes. But you want to."

He laughed. "Of course I do. How could I not? But I'm not going to, my sweet, even if you beg me."

Prudence gave a gurgle of laughter at such absurdity. "I shan't beg you," she promised.

"No, I didn't think you would."

He turned her around and she kept her eyes on his, but she could feel his male member pressed against her stomach. And then he took one breast into his mouth again and she felt her body arch against him, felt his hardness leap with the same excitement that she felt at the pull of his lips and her eyes flew to his. "I see," she said.

"Yes, I thought you would. It's nothing to be afraid of, any more than I would be alarmed by your arousal. They're perfectly natural states for a man and a woman to be in. Shall we finish taking off your shift?"

Prudence blinked uneasily at him. "But, William, I have my courses. I would be a little embarrassed to remove the shift."

Since she stood before him bare-breasted, with the shift caught around her waist, he merely sighed and lifted her into the bed. When he climbed in beside her, she asked, "Have I disappointed you?"

"Certainly not. How could I be disappointed when your lovely breasts are here for me to see, and to touch." He moved his hands provocatively on her flesh, instantly calling forth the heady excitement she was becoming familiar with. "But there is more of you to touch, lovely Prudence. And I wish you will not be embarrassed for me to do so."

As he allowed his hands to wander down her body, Prudence stiffened slightly. But his stroking felt comforting along her sides and down onto her legs. When his hands moved to the insides of her thighs, she murmured a protest. Instead of removing his hands, Ledbetter brought his mouth to her breast and teased its peak with his tongue. She was so distracted by the sensations that she didn't notice that his hands had commenced a rhythmic stroking which approached the apex where her legs joined.

And then he touched her in the most private place of all and her mouth, prepared to protest, instead uttered an altogether different sound. She heard her own moan with a mixture of surprise and longing. There was something he touched that felt even more remarkable than his lips on her breast. Something that made her body writhe with a desire for more.

But his hands had withdrawn, and his lips had moved to her mouth. While his kiss was pleasant enough, it did not convey the excitement that his touch had given her. Prudence wanted him to touch her again as he just had, but he seemed unaware of her wish. He probed her mouth with his tongue and she found it exciting, but still she wanted his hands to explore her again. She was totally unable to tell him so, and knew a certain frustration with her own cowardice.

In her dilemma, Prudence reached out to her husband, her hands clasping his hips. She loved the texture of his skin, the firmness of bone under flesh. As his kiss deepened, her hands moved to cup his bottom and she found it almost as exciting as when he had touched her. The roundness of his buttocks seemed as alluring as that of her own breasts; she heard his moan of pleasure.

And his hand moved again to that intimate spot that made her almost faint with aching. As he stroked her, she kneaded his buttocks, gripping them firmly as her need rose. Her breathing came faster and everything about her seemed caught up in a heightening spiral of urgency. His mouth moved again to her breast, tugging at it as the ache tugged between her legs. Oh, God, she could not bear this need. She would burst if it weren't satisfied.

Frantic, she begged, "Ledbetter, I . . ."

And then all hell broke loose in her body. All that pent-up energy burst forth in a shattering release that overwhelmed her senses. She could hear nothing but the rushing of her blood, nor feel anything but the rhythmic response in her body. Tears seeped from her closed eyes, and Ledbetter kissed them on her cheeks.

"Are you all right, Prudence?" he asked gently.

Even as the tears streamed faster, she nodded. "I'm sorry to be such a ninny. That was astonishing. And wonderful." She opened her eyes to meet his inquiring gaze. Her voice shook a little when she said, "Thank you. I had no idea. You must think me the greatest fool in nature to be resisting an experience such as that." And then shyly, "Is it like that always?"

"It can be, with luck and patience." He kissed her forehead and wiped away the dwindling tears. "You're not distressed?"

She shook her head. "No, it was the relief that made me cry, I think. But I feel exhausted."

He laughed. "I'm sure you do. We'll go to sleep now, my dear."

"But you . . ."

"I'll be fine." He gathered her against his body, nuzzling her hair with his face. "Good night, baroness."

With a sigh she closed her eyes again and allowed her body to relax against his. "Good night, William."

# Chapter Fourteen

When he awoke in the morning, Ledbetter found himself still holding his wife. She lay softly against him, her breathing slow and regular, and he had little doubt that she was really asleep. It would, of course, take very little to waken her. And his promise had only been for the previous night, had it not? He could, in good conscience, attempt to seduce her this morning.

At the very thought his body stirred. But Ledbetter sighed and rolled away from her. Better by far to seduce his innocent Prudence in the dark of night. Her fears and embarrassment would only be heightened in the light of day.

So he climbed carefully out of her bed, donned his dressing gown, and smiled ruefully at the diamonds that still winked in her ears. Hell, he'd meant to remove them: they must have been very uncomfortable to sleep in. Her face looked relaxed, though. Her lips were slightly parted and those funny little puffs of breath escaped them from time to time. Ledbetter was tempted to bend and kiss her, but forced himself to turn away. He had a great deal to do today and he would be wise to get started.

It was another hour before Prudence stirred. The first thing she noticed was that she was still wearing the diamonds, and very little else; the second thing was that Ledbetter was not there with her in bed. That disappointed her—a little. It seemed to say that he wasn't as interested in her . . . physically . . . as he had indicated. But of course it was all to the good, because he wouldn't expect her to . . . well, be available for him.

Prudence tugged the shift back up over her naked chest even before she got out of bed. And the minute she was on her feet she reached to unhook the diamond necklace. When she held it in her hands, she gazed at it with wonder. It had not occurred to her, somehow, that marrying Ledbetter would mean that she was showered with diamonds. After all, he had married her for her money.

Hadn't he?

Frowning, Prudence laid the diamond necklace carefully in the worn case. Then she removed the earrings from her ears and placed them there as well. Perhaps they were entailed and Ledbetter hadn't the right to sell them. Not that that had stopped any family she'd ever heard of from having a paste set made and disposing of the valuable ones to meet their debts. At the very least the baron could have borrowed money against them.

Prudence shook her head, not understanding at all. There must have been any number of ways Ledbetter could have raised even as significant an amount of money as she'd brought to their marriage. Frustrated as ever by the question, Prudence rang for Tessie. Together they needed to accomplish a great deal in preparation for the party in less than a week's time.

In the early afternoon Sir Geoffrey Manning and Lady Manning arrived at Salston. It was apparent to Prudence that they had informed Ledbetter of their impending visit, but he had neglected to mention the fact to her. Which would have made little difference, except that she would have preferred to be wearing a more attractive gown in which to receive them.

As this was her first opportunity to entertain company at Salston, she would also have liked to confer with Mrs. Collins and the cook as to what tea consisted of for guests. But in the event, it hardly mattered, because the Mannings had not been there half an hour when Catherine Manning experienced the first sign of impending childbirth.

One moment she was seated quite comfortably on the red velvet chair next to Prudence's, and the next she was standing horrified in a pool of fluid. "Oh, God, I'm so sorry," she cried. "I've ruined your chair. I told Geoffrey coming out this close to my confinement might not be the best possible idea."

"So you did, my love," he replied, contrite. "We'd best start for home instantly."

His wife stared at him with understandable astonishment. "I can't ride home in a carriage, Geoffrey. Riding in a carriage would be agony if not disaster. You *know* how fast the babies come." She looked helplessly at Prudence.

"You are not to concern yourself," Prudence said, calm in the face of emergency. "I'll have a room prepared for you straightaway. Shall we send for your midwife?"

"Oh, if you would." Catherine smiled tremulously at her hostess. "Though I must warn you that she hasn't made it in time for either of the last two births."

Ledbetter looked a little pale at this announcement. "Then who delivers the baby?"

"Oh, the housekeeper did last time. The time before Geoffrey's mother was with us."

Prudence had pulled the bell cord and instructed the footman who arrived to have Mrs. Collins see that a room was prepared immediately for Lady Manning, and to have the midwife sent for. Then she turned to Catherine and hooked her arm through her guest's. "Come. I'll take you upstairs. Once we have you comfortably in bed, we'll allow Sir Geoffrey to have a word with you, if you wish."

Catherine was looking considerably distressed by her situation, but this prosaic plan seemed to relieve her. Prudence turned to her husband and said, "Ledbetter, would you have Mrs. Collins bring up a cup of tea for Lady Manning? And some toast perhaps? When she's there we'll consider what else needs to be done."

"Certainly, my dear," her husband replied, looking rather pleased with her.

Prudence refused to allow Catherine to murmur further apologies as they made their way up the stairs and down the hallway to the largest of the guest chambers. "You haven't a thing to apologize for," she assured her companion. "I shall find it immensely exciting to have a baby arrive right here at Salston. But your children will be so disappointed not to see the new babe at once."

"They will," Catherine admitted. "They've been looking forward to seeing which side gets added to—the boys or the girls."

Prudence laughed. "Well, Sir Geoffrey will just have to bring them over to see you and the child as soon as you're rested."

"But I couldn't stay here!"

"There is nothing else you *can* do," Prudence said reasonably. "Don't distress yourself. You have more than enough to concern you right now."

As a pain gripped her guest at that moment, the two paused to wait it out. Prudence had been ten when her youngest sister was born, so she was not entirely unfamiliar with the routine surrounding childbed. When they came to the guest chamber, a housemaid was just finishing setting out towels. Prudence asked her to have Tessie bring a nightdress from her own room and the girl hurried off.

"Just how quickly *do* your babies come?" Prudence asked when she saw that Catherine was having another pain.

"In less than two hours," Catherine confessed. "At least the last two have."

Prudence grinned. "Well, we shan't have long to wait, then. Let me help you out of your gown."

But Tessie arrived then and took this task upon herself, efficiently ridding the baronet's wife of her clothing and disposing her in bed in one of Prudence's soft cotton night-dresses. "I'll be pleased to help, if you'd like me to," she said. "I've been at my sister's lying-ins."

"Thank you. That would be very kind," Catherine agreed.

Prudence pulled a chair up to the bed and talked gently with her visitor until another pain came. Then she held her hand out for Catherine to grip tightly as she withstood her body's assault. "All in *such* a good cause," Prudence murmured sympathetically.

"Well, I do love the little dears," Catherine said when she was able to reply. "But I wouldn't mind having them a little less often."

At the foot of the bed Tessie cleared her throat as unobtrusively as possible. "You could, you know," she said.

Both women regarded her with astonishment.

"Forgive me." A blush stole up her face and she shrugged her shoulders. "I didn't mean to speak out of turn. Pay no heed to me."

There was a twinkle in Catherine's eyes, despite her present situation. "I don't think Geoffrey would take kindly to being denied. Nor, for that matter, would I care to deny myself."

"You don't have to—refrain," Tessie said, looking uncomfortable. "My sister said the midwife talked to her after her second came so fast on her first. Less than a year." She shrugged again and looked pleadingly at Prudence. "I don't mean to put myself forward, Lady Ledbetter. Only Jane has been so pleased at the results. It's been three years now since the last baby."

Prudence had no idea whether this was a topic she should pursue or not, but fortunately they were interrupted by a knock on the door. Tessie informed them that it was Sir Geoffrey, and at Catherine's warm smile, Tessie and Prudence left the two alone together. Out in the hall, Tessie was apologetic.

"I meant no disrespect, my lady. Only ever since Jane told me about it I've thought it unfair that so few women seem to know. And a lot of the gentlemen do, but they never admit it! It hardly seems right!"

Curiosity overcame Prudence's scruples. "What is it the gentlemen know?"

"There's something they can wear on their . . . well, you know. They call it a French letter. Jane said some of the gentry use them with their mistresses. Imagine! But not a word to their poor wives going through childbed once a twelvemonth! As though giving birth was a rare treat!"

Tessie sounded so disgusted that Prudence had to laugh. "I daresay they're only thinking of the end result, you know. Adding to their families."

Tessie snorted. "It's not as if the quality need a number of little ones to work the farm. Begging your pardon, ma'am. I know it's none of my business one way or 'tother."

"No, it isn't," Prudence agreed gently but firmly. "But Lady Manning may well benefit from our discussion. I have a feeling she won't forget, and if she's interested, perhaps her own midwife can offer her some advice."

"Yes, ma'am."

Sir Geoffrey emerged from his wife's room then, looking a little distressed. Prudence hurried over to him, asking, "Lady Manning is all right, isn't she?"

"She says so, though how she can when one of those pains grips her I cannot understand. Think you should be with her now, ma'am, if you don't mind."

"Of course not," Prudence assured him. "We'll send you word as soon as anything happens, Sir Geoffrey."

"My thanks," he said gruffly. "I know you'll take good care of her."

"We will. Please send the midwife up directly when she arrives, but we'll be fine until then." Prudence smiled and hurried past him into the bedchamber, followed closely by Tessie. They found Catherine grimacing with pain and rolling her head on the pillow, but she waved aside their concern.

"Perfectly normal," she grunted. "It's almost time, I think."

Prudence calmly advanced and removed the covers from Catherine's lower body. "The midwife hasn't arrived yet, so you must direct Tessie and me how to go on. Do you need anything?"

"Tessie might warm a blanket at the fire to wrap the babe."

"Right away, Lady Manning."

Catherine motioned Prudence closer. "Did you find out what she meant?" she whispered, indicating Tessie with her head.

"I did." Prudence frowned slightly. "You'd best ask the midwife if she knows what a French letter is."

Her guest looked mystified but smiled slightly. "To be sure I shall. I would be just as happy to have a child every *other* year. Oh!"

Prudence watched as Catherine succumbed to a fierce urge to deliver the child. To her astonishment, she could see the hair on the baby's head before the crown of the head receded once more. "Why, it's almost here. Tell me what to do."

"When I push again," Catherine said, puffing hard, "it will start to slide out. Make sure it's breathing."

Though she would have liked to ask how she would know, Prudence restrained herself and awaited the moment when the baby's head emerged from Catherine's body. And then, all by itself, the little shoulders twisted and the whole body slipped right out. Prudence turned the baby's face to her and watched the infant take a great gasp of air—and begin to wail.

"It's a girl," she said in wonder, "and she's breathing just fine."

Catherine laughed in relief and happiness. "Julia, that's the name we decided for a girl. Oh, will you wrap her in the blanket and hand her to me? Just leave the cord attached for now."

Tessie handed Prudence the warm blanket and Prudence carefully wrapped the fragile little being in its voluminous folds. She reminded herself to have Mrs. Collins search out a proper baby blanket that didn't envelop the poor little thing so overwhelmingly.

Prudence managed to tuck the large bundle at Catherine's side so the new mother could gaze into her child's face. "She's beautiful," Prudence said, "just beautiful."

Catherine touched the little cheek with a gentle finger. "And look at all that hair! None of the children have had so much when they were born. Perhaps she'll have as glorious a mass as yours one day, Lady Ledbetter."

"Surely you must call me Prudence now," her hostess insisted, blushing slightly at the compliment. "Shall I have Sir Geoffrey in now, or do you wish to await the midwife?"

"Best wait. But do go and tell him the news. He'll be fretting."

Prudence nodded and moved toward the door just as the midwife was ushered into the room by Mrs. Collins. After a quick curtsy to Prudence, the midwife shook her head with frustration. "Not again, my lady! And the groom even sprung the horses! I'm surprised you would leave home so close to your time, but there . . . Forever leaving me with nothing to do."

"I've left the last bits for you, Mrs. Rogers," Catherine assured her, grimacing. "In fact I think that's happening right now."

Delighted to be of some assistance after all, Mrs. Rogers moved briskly forward and Prudence escaped from the room. She could feel herself smiling right down to her toes, she was so delighted with the whole experience. A new life in the world! And she had delivered the babe—as much as anyone had. Mostly Catherine had done everything herself. What a remarkable afternoon!

Two months ago Prudence could not have contemplated the possibility of having a child anytime in the near future. And now here she was, married, with every chance that she would become enceinte shortly—if she managed to overcome her ridiculous fears. Or if her husband lost patience with her.

Prudence paused in the hallway to look out the window over the courtyard. She could envision children there playing with hoops and cricket bats, dogs barking excitedly, a nursemaid keeping a watchful eye. Ledbetter teaching his son the finer points of boxing, herself laughing when her daughter rolled down the sloping lawn in her good dress. They could be a close and loving family—if Ledbetter wouldn't leave her there alone, wouldn't abandon her while he continued his accustomed life in London.

Nonsense, she scolded herself. This was no time to worry about her husband's intentions. That little slip of the tongue of his at Sir Geoffrey's shouldn't conjure up such lowering concerns. Besides, today was not the day to allow one's spirits to be dampened by her familiar but unworthy thoughts of abandonment. Baby Julia had arrived, safe and beautiful, Catherine was well, and Prudence would be the one to bring the happy news to Sir Geoffrey.

Her smile returned. She withdrew her gaze from the courtyard and hastened down the stairs. Her husband and his friend were in the Gold Drawing Room, each with a glass in hand, both pacing about the room. They turned at her entrance and Sir Geoffrey started forward.

"You have a daughter, Sir Geoffrey. And Lady Manning is well and in wonderful spirits." Prudence felt the prick of tears in her eyes from an excess of emotion. "Oh, she's the most beautiful child. You may go up to them in just a very few minutes."

Ledbetter moved to shake Sir Geoffrey's hand and thump him on the back. "Congratulations, my dear fellow! How very lucky you are to have such a fine family." His gaze moved to Prudence. "And did the midwife arrive in time?"

Prudence's eyes glowed. "No. It was just Tessie and me there with Lady Manning, and it was the most wonderful experience, William. But the midwife is here now, so Sir Geoffrey need not worry."

Ledbetter's brows had risen. "You delivered the baby, Prudence?"

"I did, after a fashion. Lady Manning delivered her to me, really. She has a great deal of hair, and her name is to be Julia."

Ledbetter looked rueful. "Well done, my dear. Perhaps it won't be so very long before we have a baby of our own."

His wife met his gaze unflinchingly. "I trust that may be the case."

"Well, of course it will!" Sir Geoffrey exclaimed. "Nothing could be more likely. Do you think I could go up now?"

With her gaze still on Ledbetter, Prudence said, "Of course, Sir Geoffrey. I'll go with you."

# Chapter Fifteen

A more hectic day Ledbetter could not remember experiencing. Not two hours after the baby was born, all the Mannings' children arrived to greet the new member of their tribe. They were extremely excited about this advent of an infant sister, and, though they tried to be on their best behavior, their high spirits couldn't quite be contained.

On his wife's suggestion, Ledbetter took the boys out to the stables to release a little of their energy. He allowed each in turn up with him on his favorite stallion for a fast gallop across the unplanted fields. The experience made him long for sons of his own, much as attending the birth had obviously made Prudence long for a child.

Ledbetter had not given much thought to producing an heir. It had not been his purpose in marrying Prudence. Though, of course, he had assumed that would be the natural outcome of their marriage. And he still assumed it, despite the detour that had occurred. In fact, he felt inclined to think that tonight might be just the right time to finally seduce her, when she was keen to conceive a child of her own.

So the baron was in a rather expansive mood when he eventually escorted Geoffrey's boys back to the house. And it was the boys who discovered that their Aunt Martha had arrived at Salston as well. She was sitting with their sisters in the Gold Drawing Room, becoming acquainted with Prudence. It had been some time since Ledbetter had seen Martha for, though she lived in the neighborhood, he was a great deal less likely to visit her than her brother Geoffrey.

Ledbetter was grateful for the boys' warning. Sometimes, when he encountered Martha by accident, he was forcefully reminded of his feelings for her as a very young man. His first love, as it were. And a woman whom he might very well have married had he not been so careless of her affections.

The baron schooled his face to a pleasant, welcoming smile as he entered the drawing room. Martha's husband was standing just inside the door and greeted him a little formally. A bit high in the instep, Ledbetter had always thought, though with nothing cold about him. He shook hands with Dennison, saying what was proper, while Dennison excused their unannounced descent on Salston as being at his wife's insistence. "Couldn't keep her away when she heard the news," he admitted.

"No, indeed, I had to come, Will!" Martha exclaimed, jumping up from the chair on which she'd been perched. "Imagine Catherine giving birth here. And now you have the whole family."

She moved toward him gracefully, looking fragile and exquisite in a royal blue costume. Tendrils of blond hair framed her face, and her blue eyes danced with good humor. "And here you are married! We have just met your charming wife and wish to offer you our very best wishes."

"Thank you." Ledbetter clasped the small hand she extended to him between both of his. "Have you seen your new niece?"

"Not yet. Mother and child are sleeping." Martha withdrew her hand and cocked her head mischievously. "Geoffrey assures me he did not do it on purpose, bring

Catherine here when her time was imminent, but I told him it was a foolhardy thing to do, knowing his wife's quick deliveries."

"Yes, yes," Sir Geoffrey muttered. "I'll know better next time."

Ledbetter noticed that Prudence's gaze had switched back and forth between him and Martha, a slight frown marring her brow. Now she said kindly, "It has been a delightful experience, Mrs. Dennison. Do not scold Sir Geoffrey on my account, I beg."

"It never does the least good to scold Geoffrey, in any case," Martha assured her. "If he thinks he's right, he pays no heed. And if he thinks he's wrong, he promises never to do it again, and promptly forgets."

Ledbetter was a little surprised by Martha's high spirits. Ordinarily a fairly retiring girl, she seemed to be intent on making an impression that afternoon. And the only one she could possibly wish to make an impression on was Prudence, since everyone else had long since formed their opinion of her.

Having no real understanding of the subtleties of female behavior, this was a great puzzle to him. He would have supposed that in such a situation it would be Prudence who would attempt to shine, since she was the newcomer and the unknown quantity to their guests. But Prudence was not putting herself forward in any way. In fact, she seemed to have withdrawn a little in the face of Martha's sparkling gaiety.

"And Will," Martha continued, much to his discomfiture, "has never allowed a soul to correct him, has he, Geoffrey? From the time he was in short pants he would get that stubborn set to his face and say, 'It wasn't my fault!' Oh, you needn't shake your head, Will Ledbetter. You know very well that it's true."

"Well, you just informed everyone that I never admit to a fault, so I don't see how you should suppose I would do so now," he pointed out mildly.

"What imp has gotten hold of your tongue, Martha?" Geoffrey demanded. "Will is the finest friend a man ever had, and I'll thank you to remember it."

"Now, Geoffrey, Will knows I'm merely teasing him. The three of us have known each other forever. I'm sure he would never take offense at my little joke."

Ledbetter had not precisely taken offense. But he had disliked having Martha proclaim one of his failings to the room at large. No, that wasn't exactly true, either. He disliked having her view put forth in front of Prudence, who no doubt was already well aware of various of his deficiencies and certainly didn't need to be informed of a new one. The poor woman would begin to wonder what had possessed her to marry him.

His wife interrupted a lull in the conversation, which threatened to become uncomfortable. "For my part, I've found Ledbetter to be surprisingly accommodating," she said with a winsome smile in his direction. "Perhaps it is being newly married which has mellowed him."

"Just so," Geoffrey agreed, nodding his head vigorously. "Noticed myself how fond he is of Lady Ledbetter. Makes a difference, you know."

The baron experienced something of a shock. He watched as his wife colored slightly, and Martha's brows rose. It took Ledbetter a moment to acknowledge the import of what he was feeling. He was indeed fond of Prudence, very fond of her. But this was an awkward moment to realize that his fondness had developed into something more. He stood staring at his wife, unable to think of a thing to say, when most fortunately a footman arrived at the door to announce, "Lady Manning is awake now and would welcome a visit from Mrs. Dennison."

"Oh, delightful," Martha said, gathering up a package with what looked like a knit blanket. "Perhaps the baby will be awake as well."

With a hasty glance at Ledbetter, Prudence rose and said, "I'll show you the way, Mrs. Dennison. I do rather hope that's a wrap you've knit for the child, because we found ourselves without anything small enough. The poor thing is swallowed up by an adult blanket, I fear."

"Why, yes, it is. And I've used the softest, warmest wool the shop in Forstairs had." Martha tugged out a corner for Prudence to finger, and the two women left the room in perfect charity.

Ledbetter expelled a sigh of relief. "I think perhaps it's time for a glass of Madeira," he announced to his remaining guests. "And I'll have Jenkins bring along the London papers."

Prudence was exhausted, both physically and emotionally. She could not count the number of times she had climbed the stairs with one of the Manning children, or one of the adults. There had been three trips to the attics as well, in a vain effort to find an old crib or a trunk full of tiny little garments. Apparently Ledbetter's mother had cleared the place out, or his sister had taken keepsakes with her for her own family. In any case there was not a useful item to be found.

And then simply entertaining the children, and the grown-ups, had absorbed the remainder of her day. The house had not emptied out until after ten o'clock, an ungodly hour in the country. Only Catherine and the baby Julia remained, but they were only down the hall from her, and Prudence could hear the baby cry as she brushed her hair in preparation for bed.

Someone would be there to help Catherine—one of the maids, no doubt. But Prudence felt the urgency of the baby's cry and almost groaned when Ledbetter's knock came at her door. "Come in."

He entered as usual in his dressing gown. By now Prudence knew that he wore nothing under it and she wondered at his audacity when Catherine and the baby were only a few doors down the corridor. She felt not the least inclination to disport herself on this of all nights. "I'm burnt to the socket, William," she said.

"Ah. I wondered what that frown was about. I'm not surprised that you're worn out." He moved behind her and placed his hands gently on her shoulders, meeting her eyes in the mirror. "You were wonderful today, my dear. Truly extraordinary handling every crisis and difficulty. And you'll need a good night's sleep because tomorrow is the dedication of that ridiculous organ at the village church."

This time Prudence did groan. "Lord, I'd forgotten that. You couldn't go alone, I suppose?" she asked, only half teasing.

He grimaced. "No, I could not. After today's performance I have every confidence that you'll manage to bring everything off splendidly for me at the service."

Prudence turned around to face him. "May I ask you something?"

"Certainly."

"Were you and Martha Dennison engaged at some point?"

Obviously this was not what Ledbetter had expected. He shrugged, a little uncomfortably, and said, "Not exactly. We were very young and had something of an understanding, but nothing came of it. She met Dennison and decided to marry him. What makes you ask?"

"She has that proprietary air that women sometimes have with an old flame." Prudence cleared her throat and asked, "Were you very much in love with her?"

"I suppose I thought so at the time." He lifted her chin with his hand, regarding her curiously. "It was a very long time ago and I must not have been desperately infatuated, for I left her in the country and damn near forgot her until Geoffrey wrote that she'd gotten engaged."

A shadow passed across her face and she shifted away from his touch. "If you wouldn't mind so very much, William, I'm urgently in need of my bed. And I've told Catherine that she is to send for me if anything untoward should arise during the night."

Her husband stiffened. "Are you telling me that you'd prefer me to spend the night in my own room, Prudence?"

Unable to meet his gaze, she lowered her eyes. "If you wouldn't mind so very much. It's just . . ."

". . . that you're uncommonly tired. Yes, I see."

"And that someone might come to get me in the middle of the night. Really, it's that even more than my tiredness."

"So this exile is likely to last for the duration of Catherine's stay."

His voice sounded so cool that she shivered. "Yes, but that won't be so very long, William. Just a few days. I'm sure she'll want to be home with her family as soon as she's able to travel."

"No doubt." He stood for a long moment regarding her, and then turned away. "Very well. We should leave for church by half past eight in the morning. I feel certain Catherine will be able to manage without your presence for a few hours."

"Ledbetter . . ." she said, holding a hand out toward him.

But he was halfway to the door and didn't see it. Prudence allowed her hand to drop to her lap as she said quietly, "Good night, William."

"Good night, Prudence."

The door closed silently behind him. Prudence couldn't help but believe that she'd made a mistake. She should not have sent him away, no matter how tired she was. But even thinking about a maid coming to get her when she was locked in Ledbetter's embrace made flags of embarrassment blossom on her cheeks. She was too new at this stage of their intimacy to feel any differently. Couldn't he understand that?

No, he could not. Ledbetter was still grievously put out when he awoke the next morning in his solitary, cold bed. It did not help that he had slept poorly, or that his valet seemed to derive unholy pleasure from his banishment. Ledbetter had a good mind to turn his valet off, but fortunately he was too distracted by his other concerns to manage that small matter.

He allowed Balliot to adorn him properly for church, though he would far have preferred planning a long, hard ride on his favorite stallion to sitting patiently in the family pew for the ceremony to be over. This was the first occasion on which most of his neighbors would meet his wife, he realized, grimacing at himself in the mirror as Balliot worked with finicky fingers on the starched white cravat.

Prudence would charm everyone; she always did. She was gracious, and pretty, and eager to please. What more could a man ask in his wife? Well, for one thing, that she'd become his wife in a more tangible way than the uttering of her marriage vows.

Hadn't he been incredibly patient with her? He had. And

it had not been easy for him. Well, to be perfectly truthful, which perhaps he should attempt to be with himself, it had been a great deal easier than he would have thought. Ledbetter had found it quite enchanting to begin introducing his wife to the pleasures of the flesh. And he damn well wanted to get on with more of those lessons—to see the wonder in her eyes, and her shy excitement make the color bloom in her cheeks.

But perhaps he had misjudged her reactions. If she had been as enchanted as he, she would never have been willing to send him off to his own room last night, would she? And what would happen if her lack of interest persisted? Oh, Ledbetter knew enough of his bride to realize that she would "do her duty." But he didn't want that. He wanted more, a great deal more.

"Does my lord wish to wear his signet ring this morning?" Balliot asked hopefully.

"No, he does not," Ledbetter growled. "And he is not going to stand here one more minute while you smooth out imaginary wrinkles and whisk off nonexistent bits of fluff. Run along, man."

Offended, as only Balliot could be offended, the valet fled. Ledbetter shrugged his shoulders to ease the fit of the jacket which clung masterfully to his form, and sighed. It was going to be a long day.

At the breakfast table Prudence picked at her food.

"Are you unwell?" he asked, in a not-very-sympathetic voice.

"I'm perfectly fine, thank you."

"I trust you slept well."

"Then your trust is misplaced."

Surprised, he set down his cup. "Were you disturbed in the night? Was something amiss with Catherine?"

"No one came for me at all." She lifted troubled eyes to his and said softly, "I missed having you there with me. I'm sorry I sent you away."

"Well." Suddenly the day looked a great deal brighter to Ledbetter. "Well," he said again, uncertain how to respond. "I missed being with you."

"Perhaps," she said, her voice halting, "I could come . . . to you tonight?"

Ledbetter's breath caught in his chest. What a remarkable woman she was! "Yes," he said, "that would be an excellent solution."

"Then I shall," she said with determination.

He would have liked to shower her with kisses, but the butler arrived to announce that the carriage had been brought around to take them to church. Ledbetter frowned in exasperation, but Prudence jumped up exclaiming, "I must get my bonnet. I won't be a minute."

So he thanked the butler, finished his coffee, and rose to face the next ordeal.

Prudence felt a great deal better after she had mended her fences with Ledbetter. She had indeed spent a wretched night, all to no purpose at all. Catherine and the baby Julia had done just fine; there had been not the least need to go to them. And tired as she had been, sleep had eluded her through most of the night. Several times she had considered gathering up her courage and walking across the hall to her husband's room. But, unsure of her welcome there, she had awaited the morning to put matters right.

Ledbetter entertained her with stories of the neighborhood as their carriage bumped along the road into the village. Now even more than a few days previously the trees were beginning to show buds. But the sky was overcast, with a definite hint of rain in the air. Prudence hoped they would make it back from church before a spring rain managed to drench the area.

As he assisted her to alight from the carriage, Ledbetter said, "You haven't forgotten about the size of the organ, I'm sure, Prudence. I will have nothing further to say on that subject this morning. What is done is done. My mother meant well in donating the instrument, and I shall attempt to focus on that generosity in my remarks."

"I shall do my best to overlook anything outlandish," Prudence promised with a rueful smile.

Ledbetter produced a grin in reply, tucked her arm through his, and guided her into the old stone church.

Though they were in good time for the church service, the building was already filled to overflowing with people. Apparently the dedication of the organ had caused something of a stir in the village and the neighboring communities. Prudence could tell which was the Ledbetter family pew, as it remained empty until they seated themselves there. Even Sir Geoffrey Manning was already at church, surrounded by two of his older children and their nursemaid.

Prudence had managed to keep her gaze away from the organ until after she was seated beside her husband. She had assumed that he had exaggerated the size of the instrument, owing to his embarrassment about his mother's involvement in the fiasco. Now, when she turned her gaze upon it, she immediately caught her lip between her teeth to stifle an almost irresistible urge to giggle.

What could they have been thinking? she wondered as she surveyed the enormous instrument. Glistening pipes streamed up to the far too low ceiling. The keyboards gleamed white and black against the lush mahogany of the wooden panels. Since no one was seated at the organ, it appeared all the more imposing, as if no one was quite brave enough to challenge its immensity.

A ripple of interest whispered through the church and Prudence turned to watch the vicar climb to his pulpit. He immediately called down a blessing on the assembled parishioners, and moved straight into the dedication of the new organ. Prudence thought him oblivious to the disproportionate size of the instrument, for he confessed to his own longing for such a splendid item, and his gratification that Lady Ledbetter, the present baron's late mother, had seen fit to provide it.

When he asked the baron to say a few words on his mother's behalf, Ledbetter rose with his accustomed ease and turned to address the congregation. "My mother developed a fascination with organ music in her later years," he said. "Even when she was not well enough to attend church, she would page through her hymnal and hum melodies she remembered hearing in church, this church, throughout her lifetime. She made a study of organs and corresponded with several of the finest manufacturers of them."

Ledbetter dropped his gaze for a moment to his wife, and Prudence smiled reassuringly at him.

"My mother hoped to share her love of music with the people of this parish. By donating this handsome organ she trusted that her family, friends, and neighbors would enjoy a special musical heritage for many years to come."

Prudence became aware that people were staring beyond Ledbetter, toward the front of the church. This would not have been unusual, since that is where the organ resided, except that there was a certain amount of elbow nudging and finger pointing. To say nothing of the curious looks and urgent whispers.

When she turned to see what it was that had captured the

attention of the congregation, she found that the organist was preparing to take his seat at the enormous instrument. The excitement that vibrated through the church was not caused by the possibility that music would soon be forthcoming, however. Prudence heard Ledbetter, who had turned to witness the organist's advent, mutter something beneath his breath which sounded very much like, "The devil you say!"

Prudence herself was dumbfounded. The man who seated himself on the organist's bench was not just any other stranger, although he appeared quite unconscious of the stir he was creating. He offered Ledbetter an inquiring look, as though to ask whether he was finished speaking and ready for the organist to begin the musical portion of this event.

Ledbetter's narrowed eyes moved from the man seated at the organ to the vicar smiling benevolently from his pulpit. Prudence knew that her husband wanted more than anything to demand, "Just what is the meaning of this?" She would certainly have appreciated knowing herself. But Ledbetter, with truly remarkable self-control, said, "I shall say no more, but will allow this accomplished organist to demonstrate the instrument's unique qualities without further delay."

On saying which, he seated himself, muttering "God help us" with a fatalistic shake of his head. He reached for Prudence's hand and held it firmly on his thigh for the next half hour, while the "accomplished organist" displayed his talents.

And they were many, Prudence had to admit. She had never heard anyone play so well, even during her Season in London. The young man, who could have been Ledbetter's twin, was no novice on the instrument. In fact, he was so good that he was able to tame the huge instrument into not overwhelming the little church with its glorious sound.

Prudence couldn't help but steal glances between her husband's face and that of the young man. The eyes, the cheekbones, the chin, the mouth, everything so very similar. The stranger had hair of a darker shade, and it curled engagingly all over his head, while Ledbetter's was much straighter. The two men were of a height, and even of an age, Prudence would have guessed. Surely not more than a year could have separated them. How could that be? Could two unrelated men look so much alike? And if they were related—how?

# Chapter Sixteen

When the church service proceeded with its usual complement of hymns, the young man, whom the vicar proudly referred to as Mr. Youngblood, played with an energy that had the villagers raising their voices quite melodiously in song. Prudence found herself singing with the others, and, after an initial hesitation, Ledbetter joined in.

But Prudence was envisioning the gatherings after the service, that time when neighbor spoke to neighbor, when the news and gossip spread from family to family. Ledbetter was not going to appreciate being the object of everyone's astonishment at the similarity of countenance he shared with Mr. Youngblood. It was bad enough that the organ's size made it a subject of some amusement; that the organist was a dead ringer for Lady Ledbetter's son was way beyond coincidence.

There was fire in Ledbetter's eyes. Prudence had no doubt he was spoiling for a fight. And she did not blame him for the way he glared at the vicar. Mr. Hidgely was certainly responsible for inviting the organist to play at the dedication service. Prudence could only assume he had chosen to do so from some deep-seated antipathy toward Ledbetter. What other explanation could there be?

But she was new to the parish and unfamiliar with the history between the vicar and Salston. Would it be taken for granted by the villagers that Mr. Youngblood was some by-blow of the late baron's? How very unfortunate. And Ledbetter would only add fuel to the fire by engaging the man of God in an angry exchange after the service.

Prudence beckoned urgently to Sir Geoffrey as the congregation rose to leave the church. Ledbetter's friend was instantly at her side, sharing a worried look with her before clapping a hand on the baron's shoulder and saying, "Hope Catherine and the child were no bother last night."

Forced to bring himself back from wherever his angry thoughts had taken him, Ledbetter said, "Of course they weren't. Damn it, Geoffrey, what's the meaning of this?"

His friend shook his head. "Couldn't say for certain. We'll get it straightened out, Will, but not now."

"Why not now?" Ledbetter asked angrily.

"Because," Prudence said calmly, tucking her hand into the crook of his arm, "you have your new bride to introduce to your neighbors, Ledbetter. That is your first obligation, now that the organ has been dedicated. I trust you won't embarrass me by relegating me to a lower priority than that of an upstart organist."

His eyes still blazed and she could see him struggle to gain control over his very natural desire to call the vicar to account for this outrageous display. But Prudence held Ledbetter's gaze with her own for the long seconds it took him to thrust his choler into the background—hardly forgotten, but tamed for the nonce.

He drew a deep breath and almost managed a smile. "You're quite right, as usual, my dear. Come. Let me make you known to your new neighbors."

And so he did, with an admirable conscientiousness that included every man, woman, and child who remained within the vicinity of the church. If a neighbor showed some tendency to divert conversation from the baron's recent marriage to the strange events of the morning, Sir Geoffrey would invariably interrupt to ask, "And have you heard my news? Catherine presented me with a baby girl yesterday—at Salston."

Only the very brave indeed were willing to attempt bringing the subject back to Ledbetter's look-alike a second time, and Prudence would merely smile and say, "We're so pleased that you enjoyed the music. Such a magnificent organ!"

Before Ledbetter had a chance to consider whether he could now in good conscience attack his second order of business, Prudence edged him toward the carriage, Sir Geoffrey insisted that he not keep the horses standing, and he found himself seated beside his bride on their way back to Salston. "I haven't finished with this matter," he grumbled.

"I know you haven't."

"But you were right to get me away from there now," he admitted, putting an arm around her shoulders and drawing her against him. "Perhaps we should retire to my room when we reach Salston."

Prudence blushed, but shook her head. "I'm sorry, William, but you must realize that Sir Geoffrey and his brood are likely to descend upon us at any moment."

"God help us," he muttered, for the second time that morning.

Ledbetter took Sir Geoffrey aside during the afternoon to discuss the strange occurrences of the morning, but his friend was unable to shed much light on the situation. "There have been rumors," Sir Geoffrey said, "of a man bearing a marked resemblance to you. I hadn't seen him before, and frankly, I'd discredited them."

"To me, he looks more like my father, but I suppose that is merely my own reluctance to admit my countenance is not as unique as I'd always assumed. It's odd knowing some other soul walks around with a face so like mine."

"Not much doubt he's related to you. Hate to think of it, though. Your father—may he rest in peace—always seemed so devoted to your mother."

"He was," Ledbetter said with conviction. "But his explosions frightened her, too, and he was impatient with her cowering. He couldn't understand how she could think he would harm her."

Sir Geoffrey grimaced. "Hell, when he went into one of his rants, it was hard to imagine he wouldn't hurt someone. You don't need to tell me that he never did, Will. I know that well enough. But his temper!"

"Terrifying." It was easy enough for Ledbetter to remember his father's explosive temper. The shouting and fist-banging had created a lasting impression on him as a child. No matter how impatient he himself became, he had promised himself never to behave in such a fashion. But the scene in church that morning had provided him with a real challenge to his worthy intentions. He could still feel the anger gnawing at him.

"But why would the vicar involve himself in such an egregiously stupid ploy as bringing in my father's bastard child to play the organ? Hell, Geoffrey, the living is in my gift. I have a good mind to kick him out."

"Of course you do, but it wouldn't look good, Will. Besides, there's obviously more to this man than meets the eye. May I make a suggestion?"

Ledbetter snorted. "When have you ever hesitated, my friend? Go ahead. Tell me some appalling truth that I'll have to live with."

Sir Geoffrey hesitated. "It's not as simple as that. It concerns your wife."

The baron stiffened. "Careful, then. I would not welcome any disagreeable comments about my wife."

"You misunderstand me, Will. What I am suggesting is that if you have not been completely frank with Lady Ledbetter, perhaps now is the time to rectify that."

"Frank about what?"

"About your mother's will."

"It could be a delicate matter to raise with my bride."

"And yet, if she doesn't understand the situation, how are you going to approach her for advice?"

Ledbetter's brows rose. "I beg your pardon?"

"Look, Will, what I'm trying to say is that your wife seems to have a very level head on her shoulders. You could do worse than seek her opinion on how to handle what has happened."

"What you're saying," Ledbetter informed him with asperity, "is that I'm a hothead and likely to go off half-cocked given the smallest chance."

Sir Geoffrey grinned at him. "Something like that. No, no, there's no need to come to cuffs over it, dear fellow. I give you credit for marrying a woman who appeals to your better nature. Though my acquaintance with Lady Ledbetter is short, I have every confidence in her capability and her judgment. She married you, didn't she?"

"Trying to puff me off now, are you?" Ledbetter sighed. "She only married me because she has three more sisters to be brought out, and two of them were very impatient to be given their chance."

Sir Geoffrey looked skeptical. "I doubt that was her reason any more than yours was her dowry, Will. But I'll say no more on that head. The two of you will have to sort that out for yourselves. Just promise me you won't do anything in a temper about the vicar and this Youngblood fellow."

"And lose your profound respect for my judgment?" the

baron grumbled. "Heaven forfend. This matter deserves some finesse, which, I may remind you, I am occasionally capable of."

"You are," Sir Geoffrey agreed, "when you let your head, and not your irritation, rule your actions."

"I have every right to be irritated."

"True, but much good it will do you to act on it. You know I'm right, Will."

Ledbetter grimaced. "Everyone but me seems to be right these days. I liked it better when they weren't."

"Maybe they always were," Sir Geoffrey suggested, a twinkle in his eyes.

"If they were, then I liked it better when I didn't know that."

Sir Geoffrey laughed and picked up his gloves from the table in the entry hall where they'd ended their walk. "I'm glad you're back, Will. Hope you'll stay around for a while this time."

Ledbetter shrugged. "We'll see how things progress."

Heeding Geoffrey's advice, Ledbetter raised the issue of his mother's will when he and Prudence were alone at dinner. "It proved to be a great surprise to me," he said.

"How so?"

Ledbetter made an all-encompassing gesture with his hand. "Salston is entailed, of course. When my father died and I came into the title, I inherited the whole of it. At least, that was what I believed."

Frowning, he took a sip of his wine and sat rolling the glass between his hands. "My mother was a local girl. Her father had no sons, so she was dowered with a large piece of land that bordered on Salston. Over the years it has become a valuable part of the estate."

"In what way?" his wife asked.

"Well, for one thing, my father had the dower house built there. Salston's original dower house had burned to the ground decades ago, and it seemed fitting to him to build the new one on my mother's land."

"Obviously your mother never lived there. Has it been empty?"

"No, mostly it's rented out to some family or other, so that it brings in sufficient revenue for its upkeep. I'll show it to you one day soon."

"I'd like that."

Ledbetter nodded. "But I was explaining about my mother's will. The piece of property was actually hers to dispose of, because it wasn't part of the entailed estate. Her will had been made many years ago, when my father was living, and it left the piece of property to me."

"Naturally."

"So one would think," he said, a plaintive note creeping into his voice. "I had no idea my mother had made a more recent will. She never spoke of it to me, though I was here the entire last month of her life."

"Tell me, William, was she perfectly lucid all that time?"

Her question startled him. "Why do you ask?"

Prudence shrugged. "Sometimes when people do unexpected things, it is because they are not quite themselves."

"I see. Well, for the most part she seemed perfectly fine, mentally. She was in a good deal of pain from her disease but the doctor did his best to alleviate that for her. And sometimes when she'd had a great deal of laudanum she would—have visions or something. She thought people were there who weren't, or she heard things that no one else could hear. That sort of thing."

"And surely she didn't make her will during those times."

"No, the will had been made several months before that."

"Did she have a solicitor draw it up?"

"Yes, but not the solicitor the family customarily used."

Prudence shook her head. "Of course not. Otherwise you would not have been surprised by its contents."

"I suppose not." Ledbetter regarded her curiously. "You seem to understand a great deal about such things."

"I've had a certain amount to do with wills and settlements recently," she reminded him.

"Yes." He sat silent for a long moment, contemplating his wineglass. At length he took up his story again. "My mother's will made two provisions that were unexpected. One was the gift of the organ to the village church. The other was that she left the piece of land she'd brought to her marriage to Mr. Youngblood."

Prudence's eyes widened. "The man who played the organ in church today?"

"I believe so, though I had never seen him before."

"But why, William? How had she come to know him?"

He gave an irritable shrug of his shoulders. "Who knows? I was not even aware that there was a connection between the two provisions of her will until this morning. They seemed entirely different matters. And then this man Youngblood appears to perform on the very organ my mother donated to the church."

"But he's not just any man, William. He bears a striking resemblance to you."

"I realize that." He shook his head in frustration. "The assumption is—and you will pardon my plain speaking, I trust—that Youngblood is my father's bastard child. Certainly the village folk are going to believe that. What's more, I think my mother must have believed it, Prudence."

"Did her will say nothing about the man? Make no comment as to why she was making such a provision?"

Ledbetter frowned. "There was some explanatory sentence, but it made no sense. She said that her act was intended to right a wrong which had taken place. Nothing more. Now I can see that the wrong she was attempting to right must have been providing for my father's illegitimate child. But I find it difficult to believe my father capable of either consorting with a woman other than my mother, or of neglecting the child of such a union, had there been one."

"And how did your mother come to know of his existence?" Prudence wondered. "Do you suppose that he approached her on his own? Possibly when she was sick and vulnerable? Or perhaps it was the vicar, who seems a deal too smug about this whole matter not to have been involved in some way."

"The vicar," Ledbetter growled, "has a great deal to answer for."

"Hmmm. I think perhaps you should allow me to handle the vicar."

Ledbetter regarded her with astonishment. "My dear girl, this is not your problem."

"No? I am married to you, William. And what's more, I think perhaps my dowry went to pay your mother's 'debt' to Mr. Youngblood."

The baron flushed. "I couldn't give him the land, Prudence. Besides, the dower house was on it now, making it a great deal more valuable than it had been when my mother brought it to her marriage. The courts agreed that I could provide Mr. Youngblood with an equivalent sum of money, that under the circumstances that particular piece of land should remain with the estate."

"And you didn't meet Mr. Youngblood during all this time?"

"No. I had no wish to do so. Wrangling over the matter has taken the better part of a year. I could have mortgaged the estate to get the necessary blunt, but Salston has never been mortgaged, and I didn't wish to be the first Ledbetter to do that."

"So you married me."

"Prudence . . ."

"It's all right, William. I knew, of course, that you married me for my dowry."

He reached across and took her hand. "It made a convenient excuse."

"I beg your pardon?"

"Hell, Prudence, I could have borrowed the money from Harriet's husband. He offered. Or taken the stupid mortgage. It wouldn't have been that difficult to pay it off in time. Salston is a thriving estate."

"So I've noticed."

He smiled at her. "Couldn't figure out what I needed the money for, could you?"

"No. Gambling debts seemed the only possibility."

"I don't gamble. Well, no more than anyone would at a loo party. Seems a useless way to throw money down a drain."

"Just what is it you're telling me, William?" she asked, her large eyes blinking uncertainly at him.

"That I came to Colwyck to ask you to marry me because I had been disappointed when you chose what's his name over me four years ago." He raked his fingers through his hair. "I didn't understand that, Prudence. He was a nice enough man, but—well—a little dull. At least it seemed so to me!"

A defensive frown stiffened her face. "He was not dull! He was very kind, very considerate of me. He was a gentle man, not in the least frightening."

"Was I so frightening?" he asked, stunned.

Confused, she shook her head, then stopped and nodded. "Yes, you were a little frightening to me, William."

"In what way? Surely my rank wouldn't have intimidated you. I cannot believe that I allowed my impatience any sway in your presence. How did I frighten you?"

Prudence made a dismissive gesture, but a slight flush had stolen into her face and she was unable to meet his eyes. "You just did," she said.

Ledbetter cocked his head at her. "Did it have something to do with your fears about intimacy?"

Though she didn't answer, she attempted to withdraw her hand from his clasp. Instead of allowing it to go, he drew her fingers up to his lips and kissed them. "But anyone you married, even what's-his-name, would have expected you to share his bed."

"I know." Her voice was only just above a whisper. "But you . . . You seemed so . . . so ready to carry me off to your lair."

"My lair!" Ledbetter couldn't help but laugh. "My poor sweet. You thought I would ravish you without a thought to your sensibilities, eh?"

"Something like that." She shyly met his amused gaze. "It was no laughing matter for me, William. I was drawn to you, but alarmed, all at the same time. Allen seemed so much safer, so much softer. Your eyes used to blaze when you looked at me."

"Don't they anymore?"

She laughed. "Yes, but I . . . I rather like it now."

"Do you?"

"Mmmm. When you came to Colwyck and seemed intent on marrying me for my dowry, I thought perhaps I had mistaken your . . . your passion. I thought it might be safe to marry you. Well, perhaps that's not quite true. I knew I had to marry so that Elinor and Gladys could be brought out, and I already knew you—a little. You had courted me when I was in London; the fact that you approached me again seemed to speak for your real regard."

"And not just for your dowry." Ledbetter toyed with her fingers, stroking them with decided intent. "I have a very real regard for you, my dear. Never doubt that. But I must admit to still wishing to carry you off to my lair."

Prudence smiled tremulously at him. "I don't find the thought of your lair so alarming anymore. I believe I had agreed to come there of my own volition tonight."

"You had," he said, rubbing her fingers against his cheek. "And I was especially pleased with your offer. Surely it must be time to retire by now."

"Nonsense. You haven't even finished your meal. And then I should visit Catherine for a while, and then we could perhaps read a chapter or two of *Emma*, and then . . ."

"And then," he said firmly, "my lair awaits."

"As you say, my lord."

# Chapter Seventeen

Prudence could not help but feel a little nervous as she crossed the hall to Ledbetter's room. She knew that tonight there would be no more putting off the consummation of their marriage. Her husband had been extremely patient with her, and she would not care to ask for any further indulgence. A part of her was even impatient to have this particular burden behind her. After all, she could not conceive a child if she remained a virgin. And after seeing Catherine with the baby, she was most desirous of having a child of her own.

That was not, of course, the only facet of the matter that she considered as she knocked hesitantly on Ledbetter's door. Even as his voice called to her to come in, she felt a shiver of apprehension twist through her. One didn't, after all, lose all one's fear simply because there were reasons to set it aside. This particular fear had somehow become deeply embedded in her. Foolish, certainly, but nonetheless real.

Prudence had rather imagined that her husband would be waiting for her naked in his room, standing there in all his unclothed male glory. Perhaps even with the evidence of his desire all too obvious. But in the dim light from the candle by his bed she could see that he was sitting up against the headboard with a book in his hand.

As he laid the book aside, he smiled at her and said, "That

was just in case it took you an especially long time to work up the courage to join me here, my dear."

"I promised I would come."

"I know you did, and I never doubted that you would. Come, Prudence. Try not to be alarmed. By now you should trust that I have no wish to frighten or harm you. Do you believe that?"

"Yes," she said softly, stepping bravely toward his bed. "You've given me every proof of your kindly intentions."

"Well, I have other intentions, too." His eyes gleamed brightly in the candlelight, filled with desire. He drew her down to sit on the edge of the bed. His fingers traced the oval of her face and lingered on her lips. "You're so lovely, Prudence."

"Thank you." She reached a tentative hand to stroke his cheek and he turned his face to kiss her palm. She could feel the barely restrained urgency that flowed from him. Her palm tingled with the heat of his need. Her body tensed, and he shook his head.

"Remember, Prudence. Remember how you can feel." He drew her toward him and captured her lips with his.

In his kiss, too, she could feel the power of his desire. As his kiss deepened, she felt threatened by the enormity of his passion. He would be swept away by it, governed by its uncontrollable recklessness. He would be driven by that overwhelming need to take her, to claim her body to satisfy that hunger that had been building for heaven knew how long.

Well, let him, she thought. Just let it run its course, get it over with.

Ledbetter drew back, frowning. "Prudence, what's the matter?"

"Nothing. Don't stop, William. I'll be fine."

Her husband gave an impatient sigh. "Not in that frame of mind you won't. Hell, I thought we'd worked this out."

"We have. I tell you there's no problem. Please just proceed."

He made a low growl of frustration. "Very well. Take off your nightdress and climb into bed, wife."

Prudence blinked unhappily at him, but did as he demanded. She dropped the nightdress on the floor, her back turned to him, and quickly worked her way under the coverlet, where she lay stiff as a board. Ledbetter was still sitting up in bed, glaring at her, so she closed her eyes. Prudence heard him snuff the candle and prepared herself for his touch.

Nothing happened.

She felt him settle down into the bed, as far away from her as he could possibly manage. "Really, William," she whispered. "It's all right."

Her husband said nothing.

"I'm sorry. Truly I am. I don't mean to be so stupid. Just go ahead and get it over with."

Ledbetter merely growled.

Prudence could have wept. She'd made a mess of things again, and all because of her idiotic, and probably quite unrealistic, fears. Why hadn't she merely kissed him back, as she had done the last time they were in bed together? That had been an entirely pleasurable—even exciting—experience. And now she'd offended her husband. Not only rejected him, but proved to him that she didn't really trust him at all. What a sorry excuse she was for a wife!

Well, matters could not remain thus. She must do something to sort this out, and if Ledbetter wouldn't speak to her, or take action, Prudence decided that she must. Carefully she inched her way over until she was close enough to touch Ledbetter. Since his back was to her, she placed a tentative hand on his hip. There was no response, not even that frustrated growl of his.

Prudence brought her body up closer to his, at first with just her own hip pressed against his bottom, but that caused no reaction, either. How could he ignore such a brave move on her part? Surely he must know what it cost her in determination to bring her vulnerable body so close to his!

With her heart pounding in her throat, Prudence shifted so that her whole body pressed against the length of Ledbetter. Her head fit in the curve of his neck, her breasts pressed against his back, and her lower body wrapped around the firmness of his buttocks. She rested one hand on his hip and, because it seemed a tempting thing to do, after a while she stroked his hip and thigh.

There was a decided reaction to this move on her part. Ledbetter captured her hand and refused to release it. Still he said nothing, however. She would have thought he'd be glad of her stroking him! He seemed to like nothing better than stroking *her*!

Prudence found that her body longed to be stroked. Her naked breasts against his back seemed to remember the feel of his hands on them. She shifted so that her breasts rubbed gently against his skin, and again. Where were his hands to cup them? Where was his mouth to take her nipple in and suckle it? The sensations he had aroused in her on previous occasions were prickling at her memory and in her bosom. Is this how he felt when she was close to him?

She kissed his neck, and his shoulders. The sensation of need for his touch grew deeper, and she allowed it to find expression in those hungry little kisses. She continued to rub her breasts against his back, to offer them some desired stimulation. Her body felt shockingly ripe with desire.

"Will?" she whispered near his ear. "I want you to touch me. I need you to touch me."

Her husband shifted now, turning over to face her. In the darkness, even with her eyes adjusted to the night, she could not read his face well. He seemed to study her for a long time. "I don't want any sacrifices from you, Prudence."

She silently shook her head. He had released her hand to roll over and she brought it to his thigh, allowing it to stroke him in the way she wanted him to stroke her.

Tentatively, he brought a hand up to stroke her cheek, and, as he had done earlier, she turned her face to kiss his palm. He cupped her face in both his hands and stared deeply into her eyes. Prudence didn't flinch away from his scrutiny, or from the kiss he gave her next. It was a gentle kiss, lacking the searing passion of his previous kisses. Prudence responded with quite a different kiss, one filled with all the longing she was feeling. When her husband deepened his kiss, she met his desire with a matching need.

His hand came to cup her breast and she sighed with pleasure. His gentle stroking excited her, making her slightly breathless. When he lowered his mouth to take one nipple in and draw on it, a pleasure so great overcame her that she moaned. And the tingling in her body seemed to radiate lower as he kissed and suckled her breast, until her whole body felt filled to bursting with a glorious need.

She realized now that he had been stroking her thigh as she stroked his. And his hand moved now between her legs. For the briefest of moments she felt herself stiffen, and then she spread her legs to welcome his stroke on her inner thigh. His hand paused and he said, "Do you want me to touch you there, Pru?"

"Yes. Now."

He laughed. She could feel the rumble of it through his body, a surprisingly sensuous experience. He said, "If something doesn't feel good, just say so, my sweet."

"It feels—marvelous." And indeed it did. His fingers had reached the apex between her legs and continued to stroke there, surprising her with the intensity of her reaction. She felt almost giddy with the sensations that coursed through her body. His mouth on her breast, his fingers rubbing a most sensitive spot, Prudence could scarcely breathe. Her body, which had felt ripe before he even touched her, now felt close to bursting.

She could feel his manhood straining against her leg, and knew that his passion was as highly aroused as her own. His fingers slipped inside her and she froze.

He sighed. "Ah, Prudence, please trust me."

"I *do* trust you," she said fiercely. "It's myself I don't seem to trust, Will. Believe me."

He withdrew his fingers from inside her and she caught his hand. "Please, it felt so good a moment ago. Would you do that again?"

"With pleasure," he said, kissing her forehead and beginning to stroke again at that point between her legs that made her feel giddy.

"Oh, yes," she whispered. "I can hardly bear how exciting that is, Will. It makes me feel like . . . Oh." She moaned, her body writhing beneath his touch. "Oh, God. I think I'm going to burst. Oh, Will."

She clasped him to her as her body convulsed with the most astonishing rhythmic pleasure, releasing all that amazing pent-up tension. She cried out and felt tears stream down her cheeks. "Please, please, make me yours, Will," she whispered against his throat.

He shifted her beneath him and plunged his manhood into her so swiftly that she hardly realized what was happening. There was a moment of sharp pain, followed by a lesser discomfort as he thrust into her again and again until he cried out in release.

They were joined in a way that mesmerized Prudence. She'd had no concept of how it would feel to have an empty part of herself filled by a part of her husband. As Ledbetter lay on top of her, he shifted his weight slightly to one side, leaning on his elbow and looking down at her. With his other hand he rubbed away the moisture on her cheeks.

"Are you all right, Prudence?" he asked, his brow drawn down with concern. "Should I remove myself?"

"Oh, no. Please don't." Prudence hugged her arms tightly around his back. "Stay with me."

He kissed the tip of her nose. "Not as bad as you'd feared, eh?"

She shook her head. "I've been such a fool. Can you forgive me?"

"There's no need. I daresay I'm as relieved as you are to have this first time behind us. It won't hurt from now on. And there's so much to explore. You have the most delicious body."

He kissed the swell of her breast, his tongue circling her nipple, his lips tugging gently at it. "Your body can offer you extraordinary pleasure—as it does me."

A soft moan escaped her. "Can we do it again?" she asked.

Ledbetter laughed and kissed her softly on the lips. "Not right away, my sweet. And I'm afraid you'll be sore for a while, perhaps a day or two. Best to let that heal, given your fears about pain."

"But I won't worry about that—*now*. Don't you think we'll want to . . . to try it again tomorrow night?"

"Well, we probably would," he admitted, grinning at her, "but I'm going to be off in the morning, so that will serve as a useful separation until you heal."

Prudence's heart sank and her voice had a slight edge to it when she asked, "But where are you going, William? You hadn't said anything about leaving."

Her husband shrugged as he withdrew from her and rolled over to the side of the bed. "I have some matters to clear up, concerning Mr. Youngblood, mainly. I won't be away long, Prudence. After all, we're giving a dinner for the neighbors in a few days."

She was silent, trying to reason with herself about this revelation. It was not, she assured herself, that he had only stayed around long enough to make her his wife in more than name. There was indeed something havey-cavey about the business with Mr. Youngblood, and of course Ledbetter would be anxious to set matters right. "But you've already used my dowry to settle your debt with Mr. Youngblood, haven't you?" she asked.

"Yes," Ledbetter admitted. "I doubt there's any way I can retrieve that, and in time the estate will absorb the cost. But I *have* to know the answers to a number of questions, Prudence. There is a suspicion in the air about my father which I should try to clear."

Prudence pulled the coverlet up to her chin and regarded him with a frown. "And what if you were to find that the suspicion was correct? What would you do then?"

"I don't know," Ledbetter said irritably. "There won't be much I *can* do, I'm afraid. Don't worry that any of it will reflect on you."

"That is not my fear," Prudence said, an indignant catch in her voice. "If, after all, your father wronged Mr. Youngblood, then your mother has certainly done her utmost to right the wrong. If, on the other hand, Mr. Youngblood has not been wronged, but has played upon your mother's sympathies, then perhaps you will be able to find some remedy in the law. In either case, my dear Ledbetter, I don't understand how rushing off is going to provide the answers to your very natural questions. You would probably do as well to begin your search here, where your father lived all his life."

Ledbetter expelled a snort of frustration. "I've already

done what I could in this neighborhood, Prudence. No one is going to admit to me that my father sowed his wild oats right here in the county. You'd think for all I've been able to discover that he was a paragon of virtue—which I can tell you he was not! No, I'm going to dig around where Youngblood currently lives, see what I can find there. Can't you see that it's my responsibility to discover the truth?"

Prudence sighed, and forced herself to speak without a trace of the disappointment she felt. "Certainly I can, William. You owe it to both your parents, and to yourself, of course. If you have exhausted the possibilities around Salston, naturally you must travel farther afield. I shall miss you, of course, but I will have Catherine's company for the next few days."

"Very true," he said heartily. "You and Catherine seem to go on well together. Perhaps she can stay until I return."

"I don't think she will wish to stay at Salston any longer than is absolutely necessary. She will want to be back in the bosom of her family."

"I know Geoffrey wants her home. Well, you'll be busy after she leaves, getting ready for our guests. That always seems to take a great deal of planning and consulting with Cook, and with Mrs. Collins. I daresay you'll scarcely notice I'm gone."

"Oh, I'll notice," she said, her voice soft and a little whimsical. "But I'm used to being left behind."

If Ledbetter wondered what she meant by that, he had the good sense not to question her. Instead he leaned across and kissed her. "Good night, Prudence. When I return," he promised, "we'll take up where we left off tonight."

"I do hope so."

Catherine pronounced herself well enough to endure the carriage ride to Hawthorne Manor a day and a half after

Ledbetter's departure. Prudence knew she would miss having mother and child with her, but she was well aware that Catherine could scarcely contain her desire to be in her own home with her husband and children around her. So she waved merrily as Sir Geoffrey handed his wife into the old-fashioned barouche, and she was a little surprised when Sir Geoffrey returned to speak with her.

"Can't thank you enough for the care you've taken of Catherine and the babe, Lady Ledbetter. Frightfully sorry to have made it necessary."

"Nonsense! I can hardly think of a more wonderful experience, Sir Geoffrey. And I appreciated the opportunity to get to know your wife better. I hope she'll be up to coming to our dinner on Saturday, but we will certainly understand if that's not possible."

"She'd like nothing better. Never one to be slowed down by a lying-in! And my mother will be here to help by then."

"Will she? Oh, please include her in our invitation. Ledbetter has the greatest fondness for your mama."

"Know he has." Sir Geoffrey shook his head. "Can't imagine why he thought he had to go haring off that way. Damnedest fellow for acting on the spur of the moment—begging your pardon. Well, he'll be back for the dinner, so he can't be gone long."

"Yes, and I've a great deal to accomplish before he returns," Prudence assured him. "You mustn't linger, Sir Geoffrey. It's starting to look like rain and I would wish Catherine home before we have a cloudburst."

Prudence was touched when Sir Geoffrey clasped her hand with firm pressure, then lifted it to his lips to kiss. "Contrary fellow," he muttered, "to leave such a lovely bride behind when you've been married so short a time."

"He felt it his responsibility to act," Prudence said gently. "I quite understand that."

Sir Geoffrey looked rueful. "Then you understand a great deal more than I do. Never mind. I'd best get my wife and child home. Good day to you, Lady Ledbetter, and our thanks again."

Prudence retreated into the house when the carriage had rolled off down the drive. Because she was a very organized woman, she had the arrangements for the dinner party very much in hand. But she had put off writing to her family since she had left on her wedding day, and she felt it was more than time to make up for that omission. Her sister Lizzie would be especially anxious to hear how she went on. While Prudence was scratching away with the quill on a fresh sheet of paper, she heard the rain begin and turned to watch it fall outside the withdrawing room window.

Somewhere out there Ledbetter was playing his version of Bow Street Runner, trying to track down clues about Mr. Youngblood's parentage. Prudence had been too distracted by her house guests and her preparations for the dinner to consider whether she might herself do any searching out of information. But as she watched the miserable rain drench the landscape, and the ink dried on her quill, an idea came to her. She rang for Tessie.

When the girl arrived and curtsied, Prudence beckoned her close. "Tessie, were you at church on Sunday?"

"Yes, my lady. With the servants, in the back. That's a very fine organ his lordship's mother gave the church."

"Yes, isn't it?" Prudence's eyes sparkled. "It would have done very well for a cathedral as well. But that's not what I'm concerned about just now. You heard Mr. Youngblood play?"

"I did. My, I've never heard music like that before, ma'am. He could play for the Prince Regent, everyone said."

"A remarkably fine performance," Prudence agreed. "But

what I wish to ask you about, Tessie, is his resemblance to
Lord Ledbetter, and the reaction of the servants to it."

"Oh, they were that astonished!" Tessie admitted, a gleam
in her eye. "Had a great deal to say about it on our walk back
to Salston."

"You walked?"

"Oh, yes, ma'am. It's a tradition, Mrs. Collins said."

"Hmm. Perhaps we should update that tradition a little.
But, Tessie, what I'd like, if you are able, is for you to tell
me what they said. Not like telling tales, you understand.
You needn't tell me who said what. But I would be very
grateful to know what their impressions were about that
likeness between the two men."

"Yes, I see." Tessie looked thoughtful. "Well, there was
those as felt he, Mr. Youngblood, was a . . . a natural child of
the old Lord Ledbetter, this one's papa, you know. Said you
couldn't find someone so alike without there being a connection. But there was others as scoffed at that, saying the
old lord weren't that kind of fellow. Got into a bit of a huff,
some of them. One, he said that weren't the way of it at all."

Prudence's interest sharpened. "And what did he think
*was* the way of it?"

"He didn't rightly say, my lady. Just that there was no call
to be thinking the old lord done anything he shouldn't
have."

"Tessie, would it be asking too much of you to tell me
who said that?"

The girl shook her head. "Don't see any harm in it,
ma'am. 'Twas the head gardener."

# Chapter Eighteen

There was little more that the girl was able to tell Prudence. Tessie was inclined not to place too much dependence on the gardener's statements, as she explained, "His hearing is none too good, my lady." Still, Mr. Newhall seemed a possible source of information. Prudence had heard Mrs. Collins say that the gardener had grown up on the estate, that no one had worked there longer. And it seemed very likely to Prudence that if Ledbetter had spoken with him, Ledbetter would already have known about the gardener's deafness.

So Prudence made a special trip to the succession houses in hopes of finding the gardener at work. The rain was coming down in earnest now, and she felt more than a little damp when she stomped into the glass-sided building, but the riot of colors immediately put any thought of discomfort from her mind.

"Oh, how beautiful," she breathed, taking in the rows of spring blooms. She could see that Mr. Newhall was going to turn her dining room into a spectacular garden for the Salston guests. The daffodils and tulips were especially promising, their blossoms so newly unfurled that they seemed to quiver with promise. A rainbow of color waved across the room, drawing Prudence down one aisle after another.

"They please, do they, my lady?" a voice asked from across the room.

Prudence glanced up to see Mr. Newhall entering from the potting room. "I've never seen anything so magnificent," she said, being careful to speak slowly and clearly. "I can scarcely wait to see them in the dining room."

"It will be a treat, it will," he agreed, grinning widely. "Haven't told his lordship, have you?"

"No," she admitted. "I want to surprise him."

"Aye. He'll be surprised."

"Have you all the help you'll need?"

"More than enough, thanks to your ladyship. I'll hardly have to lift a finger."

"Good." Prudence crossed the room toward him, her fingers straying to touch a blossom here and a leaf there. "Mr. Newhall, may I ask you a question?"

"As it pleases you," he said, though he looked wary.

"You were at church Sunday."

"Aye."

"And you saw the young organist, Mr. Youngblood."

He nodded, his brows lowering in a frown. "No missing him. Couldn't hear the music much, but I could feel it, don't you know."

Prudence thought he must mean that he could feel the vibrations of the mighty organ through his feet. "Mr. Youngblood looks a great deal like my husband."

"Aye, but you're not to be thinking the old lord sired him, ma'am, for it ain't true."

"Do you know that for a fact?"

"Near as can be," he said, his voice rough. "Knew the old lord as well as anyone, I daresay. He weren't in the petticoat line. Had a temper, and got foxed on occasion, but I'd bet my grandfather's watch that he never sired that organ-playing fellow."

Prudence sighed inwardly. It was not enough that the gardener's loyalty prevented him from envisioning Ledbetter's father as a philanderer. Newhall might very well be right, but he could hardly provide proof positive. She was about to turn away when she thought to ask, "Do you have any idea who Mr. Youngblood might be, then?"

"Aye."

Prudence stared at him. "You do?"

"Can't be certain, of course, but my guess would be that he's Francis's son."

She searched her memory for any mention of the name but could think of none. "Francis?"

"Aye. Francis Ledbetter, the old lord's younger brother. Uncle of the present baron."

"But Ledbetter doesn't have any uncles."

"May not now," Newhall ruminated. "Could be he's long dead. But he most certainly existed, Francis. Charles, the old Lord, and Francis and I all played together as boys."

Though his hearing might be impaired, there was nothing wrong with the old man's memory, so far as Prudence could tell, but his revelation astonished her. "And what became of him?"

Newhall shrugged. "Don't rightly know. The family disowned him when he ran off with one of the maids. Always was a bit of a scapegrace. Don't think he married her. This might be her son, or a son by some other woman. Francis, now he was in the petticoat line," the gardener said with a trace of envy. "And they adored him. He could sweet-talk them right out of . . . Well, excuse me, my lady. He was a handsome devil, that Francis. But he had no sense of what was owing the family name. Acted more like a stable lad than brother of a baron."

"Perhaps he resented being a younger son."

"As to that, I couldn't say. Francis came into an inheritance from his own uncle when he was twenty, and there was no stopping him after that. Charles, now, he had the po-

sition and the estate, but he also had the responsibility. Did
a fine job of improving the land and the buildings. Great pity
he had such a temper. Drove the young lord away."

Prudence asked hesitantly, "Did they argue, Ledbetter and
his father?"

The old man shook his head with rueful reminiscence.
"Like cats and dogs. William, that's to say the present baron,
took mighty exception to the old lord's way of shouting at
anyone who got in his way or slowed him down. And most
everyone did. Never knew a fellow with such a drive in him,
like he couldn't sit still for two minutes together."

"Where did Ledbetter go when he left?"

"To London, usually. When he was younger, to Sir Geoffrey's."

"I see. How long ago did Ledbetter's father die?"

"Three—four years, maybe." Newhall scratched his chin.
"Went just like everyone said he would—in a rage.
Apoplexy, the doctor said. I miss him. He used to come
down to the succession houses of a summer evening and
we'd smoke a pipe and talk about the old days. He talked
about Francis some with me, never with anyone else, don't
you see? His parents were so disgusted with the boy that
they struck his name from the family Bible and no one ever
spoke of him."

Newhall sighed and shrugged his bony shoulders. "But
we'd been lads together, like I said, and when the old lord
needed to remember the old times, he'd come to me. He
never knew what became of Francis. No one ever heard a
word from the boy after he left here."

"But Ledbetter must surely know of his existence!"

"Maybe so, maybe not. It was all water under the bridge
by the time William Ledbetter came along. And another
thirty years since then, close enough." The old man shook
his head. "Like as not, though, the organ-playing fellow de-

scends from Francis, not from Charles. Francis had that kind of curly hair."

"Thank you for telling me, Mr. Newhall." As she turned to leave, Prudence remembered her disagreement with her husband, and paused. She smiled earnestly at the gardener and said, "I hope you know how much we appreciate your skills and hard work, sir. But Ledbetter reminds me that you've worked here all your life and may wish to sit back and relax now. It's your decision, whether you'd prefer to stay on as head gardener, or retire from your duties and have a well-deserved rest. There's no urgency for an answer."

"Don't know what I'd do with myself if I didn't manage the gardens and the succession houses," he grumbled.

"Just think about it."

"Yes, ma'am. I'll do that."

The first thing Prudence did when she returned to the house was to have Mrs. Collins find the family Bible for her. And there it was in black and white, so to speak. Francis Ledbetter had been born two years after Charles Ledbetter, and his name entered on the date of his baptism. But at some point later in his life, someone had taken a pen and drawn a thick black line through his name.

Ledbetter did not seem to Prudence to be someone who would spend much time perusing the family Bible, and therefore would not likely have learned of his uncle's existence in that way. But surely his father, or his mother, or *someone* else had told the boy or the man of Francis's place in the family history. Such secrets always managed to find their way into the light of day eventually. Of course, it was always possible that Mr. Youngblood *was* the means by which this particular secret was coming to light.

Prudence set aside the Bible and looked thoughtfully out the window, where she could see that the rain was still falling in earnest. In all likelihood, this solved the problem of who Mr. Youngblood truly was. On the other hand, it did not solve the mystery of why the vicar had involved himself in the whole matter.

Ledbetter might demand that information from the man of God, but Prudence thought her husband's patience would be sorely tested by such an endeavor. Therefore, she decided to undertake the business herself, knowing that Ledbetter would not necessarily approve of or appreciate her efforts, that he might even be seriously annoyed with her.

But then, Prudence was seriously annoyed with him for deserting her there at Salston while he wandered about the countryside. It was, after all, scarcely a week since they had wed. So she could not be too distressed about Ledbetter's finer sensibilities. If he had any.

Prudence slid another sheet of parchment from the pile on her escritoire, dipped her quill in the standish, and wrote: "Dear Mr. Hidgely, I would be most grateful if you would call on me at Salston when the weather improves, as I desire a private consultation with you. Thanking you in advance, Prudence Ledbetter." She folded the sheet over, scratched his name on the outside, sealed the missive with the previous Lady Ledbetter's sealing wax, and rang for a footman.

Mr. Hidgely presented himself at Salston the next morning rather early, though the day looked almost as dreary as its predecessor. Prudence had him brought to her in her private parlor and greeted him with a slight degree of formality, because she thought he would expect it of her. She was, after all, Lady Ledbetter, the baron's new wife, and therefore about to become something of a figure in local society.

Though she suspected Mr. Hidgely accounted himself quite impervious to the privileges of rank, she suspected he was no less a social creature than any other man in the parish. His particular regard for Ledbetter's mother, enhanced by that good lady's gift of the impressive organ to his church, suggested that he was not unmoved at least by wealth and power.

After she had begged him to seat himself, and sent for tea, Prudence got down to the business of quizzing the vicar. "Have you been vicar here long?" she asked.

"A dozen years or more, my lady, brought here at the request of his lordship's father." The vicar sat relaxed in his chair. He was a man of medium height, with a rather long face and scant eyebrows.

"And did you know the family at Salston before you came here?"

He shrugged one hand which rested on the arm of his chair. "Not to say knew them, Lady Ledbetter. I was a very distant relation of the former Lady Ledbetter's, though we had never met. I'm sure she interceded on my behalf when the parish was in need of a new man."

"That was kind of her. I understand she was a devout and generous patron of the church. The organ she bequeathed is quite remarkable."

Mr. Hidgely's rather dour countenance brightened with a proud smile. "Indeed, there's not another parish church in the county which has so fine an instrument."

"Do you know how it came about that Ledbetter's mother chose to donate precisely that instrument?"

He eyed her suspiciously. "I don't take your meaning, my lady."

"She was so specific in her will," Prudence explained. "If I were planning to donate an organ to the church, I wouldn't have the first idea which one to suggest, but would simply specify that a certain amount of money be spent on an organ. But my husband's mother seems to have investigated the subject with particular vigor and chosen a specific instrument. I wondered if that had anything to do with you, or perhaps with Mr. Youngblood."

"Lady Ledbetter did not take me into her confidence on the matter," he said stiffly. "I'm sure she prayed for guidance and was answered by a higher authority."

"Or by a rather human one," Prudence said dryly. "Mrs. Collins tells me that Mr. Youngblood came on several occasions to visit my husband's mother. As he is an organist of considerable skill, I don't doubt that he had a certain amount of influence on the dowager."

"That I could not answer for, my lady. The baroness was inordinately fond of music, as anyone will tell you. She knew that the organ at our small church had been disintegrating for the last half dozen years of her life and hearing the dismal music it produced undoubtedly determined her to do something about the problem. Her choice of instrument was not made lightly, I feel sure."

"Perhaps you met Mr. Youngblood here at Salston," Prudence suggested.

"I am certain I did not."

"But you met Mr. Youngblood before Lady Ledbetter made that provision in her will, did you not?"

"My lady, I have no idea when Lady Ledbetter made the provision of which you speak. She was not well for many months before her death and seldom left the estate."

"Then it would seem that the solicitor must have come to her. I believe you know that gentleman—a Mr. Meakin of Market Stotton."

The vicar took advantage of the interruption caused by the footman bringing in the tea tray not to respond to her question. He murmured an appreciation of the variety of items being offered, and chose several of them to arrange carefully on his plate. He hesitated before taking the cream cake, but at length determined to add it to the ginger bar, the cucumber sandwich, and the cheddar tart. He asked for three lumps of sugar and accepted his cup from her without rattling it in its saucer.

Prudence allowed him to sit back comfortably and sip his tea, a blend the previous Lady Ledbetter had probably served him many times herself, as it was a specialty at Salston. He attempted to shift the conversation by discussing the many projects Lady Ledbetter had involved herself with at the parish church, but Prudence was not to be distracted.

"Is Mr. Meakin your own solicitor?" she asked, completely ignoring his conversational sally.

"I have no need of a solicitor, Lady Ledbetter. I'm a very simple man."

"I doubt that," she said, but pleasantly, helping herself to a ginger bar. "I understand that the living for the parish church is in Ledbetter's gift. So I must admit that I find your actions unaccountable. You must certainly be aware that Ledbetter does not suffer fools or mockers lightly. Weren't you afraid that he would dispossess you of your position?" She regarded him with a bright curiosity that gave no hint of the appalling frankness of her question. Mr. Hidgely shifted uncomfortably in his seat but blustered his way around the flat-out inquiry.

"Lady Ledbetter, the dowager, that is, assured me that I would have my position for as long as I wished it. I have a letter to that effect. I don't think the baron would wish to go against his mama's wishes."

"Don't you? Then I fear you are mistaken, Mr. Hidgely. Ledbetter is unlikely to be moved to obey the wishes of a parent who was being put upon in a most unconscionable manner."

"I'm sure I have no idea what you speak of," the vicar insisted.

"Do you not? Then I shall explain. It seems to me that you

took advantage of the dowager's illness and vulnerability to promote a little plan of revenge for yourself. Though I have no idea precisely what it is you wished to be revenged of, my guess would be that it had to do with some mistreatment of yourself by my husband."

The man of God stared at her, his face becoming red with heightened emotion. "You have no idea what you're saying, Lady Ledbetter! How you, who have only just arrived in this community, could accuse me of such improper conduct, I cannot imagine. Perhaps your husband has tainted your opinion of me. Certainly he has no great fondness for me or my position here."

"Can you blame him?" Prudence asked gently. "When his mother was ill and dying you introduced into her sphere a man who looked so like her son that she must certainly have thought the two men had the same father. In fact, you allowed her to believe that they did, though I suspect you know the truth of the matter, that they are likely cousins."

"This is wild speculation, my lady." The vicar rose from his chair, leaving his cup of tea half finished. "I will not listen to another word."

His hostess put up a hand to catch his attention. "Believe me, you will do better to listen to some hard truths from me rather than from my husband, Mr. Hidgely. I have a far more equable temper than Ledbetter has."

"Like father, like son," the vicar snapped. "Neither has any restraint on his tongue. The old lord once called me a jackanapes! Me, an emissary of the Church of England. And I suppose I should humble myself to him because of his title, or because he holds my living in his colicky hands! It's more than a man should be required to bear."

"Yes, it is," Prudence agreed, "but my understanding is that Ledbetter's father was even-handed in his rages. They did not fall solely on men of God, but on his wife, and his son, his staff, and anyone else who happened to be around when he was overcome with spleen. Why you should have taken his attacks so personally, or punished his wife for them, I cannot fathom."

"I did not punish his wife."

"What do you call letting her believe that her husband had sired a son out of wedlock?"

"I am not responsible for what Lady Ledbetter believed," he said self-righteously.

"I disagree. In your attempt to avenge yourself for the bad temper of a dead man, you introduced his widow to Mr. Youngblood. Or perhaps you reconciled yourself to what you were doing by convincing yourself that Ledbetter was just as bad as his father, and he was the one who would have to see to the carefully planned disposal of a large and prosperous portion of his estate. He was the one who would have to purchase that ridiculously large organ and hear it played in the church in front of his family and friends by a man who looked his very twin."

"Nonsense."

"Mr. Hidgely, do you deny that you introduced Mr. Youngblood to Lady Ledbetter?"

The vicar pursed his lips, his eyes hard. "She had a right to know of his existence."

"Why? Did you really believe him the old lord's child?"

"What else was I to think?" he demanded, defensive. "He looks the image of his father."

"But did he present himself to you as old Lord Ledbetter's natural child?"

The vicar hesitated, obviously torn about how to respond. "I believe I've answered a sufficient number of your questions, my lady. If you will excuse me . . ."

"But I won't." Prudence kept her voice firm but neutral. "Let me remind you that between us we may come to some benign resolution of these matters, Mr. Hidgely. If you are forced to deal with Ledbetter, I think I can promise you that your chances of remaining vicar at Forstairs are relatively small. On the other hand, I have every wish to smooth over this most unpleasant episode. Please sit down."

Grudgingly, Mr. Hidgely returned to his chair, but he ignored his cooling cup of tea and retained a look of mulish obstinacy. Prudence repeated her question.

"Mr. Youngblood came to me with a desire to be made known to the family at Salston. He believed himself related to the Ledbetters, though his tale of a disinherited younger son seemed pure fabrication to me."

"Ah, then he does know he is Francis's son, and not the old lord's."

"I had never heard of Francis. Not one word since I came to this parish as vicar."

"You could quite easily have looked it up in the parish church records. And I imagine that you did."

He rubbed his forehead as though it had begun to ache. "Indeed I did. The fact that Francis had existed did not necessarily make Mr. Youngblood his son."

"It must certainly have seemed probable, since he claimed that he was."

"Yes, yes, of course it did. But I had already introduced him to Lady Ledbetter by that time, and she was quite taken with his plight. She was also fascinated by his claim to be a musician. Apparently she held talent of that sort in very high regard, having been quite hopeless herself in playing even the pianoforte."

The vicar spread his hands in a helpless gesture. "I could not very well disillusion her once she had taken to him that way. And, besides, who was to say that his tale was the truth? He might very well have been old Lord Ledbetter's natural son, and merely been raised with the belief he was son to the disinherited brother. In either case he was illegitimate, and obviously of Ledbetter blood. Didn't it make sense that the Ledbetter family should take care of him?"

"I imagine my husband would have been perfectly willing to make an allowance to Mr. Youngblood if he had been approached with the young man's claim to a family connection. What you did, Mr. Hidgely, was an act of petty revenge against the short-tempered Ledbetters because they had managed to offend you. Only if you are willing to accept responsibility for your actions is Ledbetter likely to consider forgiving you. You undoubtedly gave his mother a great deal of unnecessary distress, something you could have easily rectified when you discovered the truth."

"But I did not . . ." Mr. Hidgely closed his mouth with a snap of his teeth and stared down at his hands for some moments. Eventually he sighed and lifted his gaze to Prudence's patient observation. "You are quite right, of course. I could have relieved her mind. I *should* have relieved her mind. But by the time I felt absolutely certain of the truth of the matter, Lord Ledbetter had returned to Salston and I hadn't the courage to present myself here."

He waved a dismissive hand. "I told myself that her ladyship was too ill to be bothered with the entire matter again. I was aware that she had sent for the solicitor to change her will. I could have intervened, and I didn't, largely because the old lord's words still rankled with me."

"Do you think you could explain that to Ledbetter—and apologize to him?"

"I shall have to, shan't I? It was a very unchristian thing to do."

Prudence smiled a little sadly. "We all make mistakes, Mr. Hidgely. I believe you will find that Ledbetter is of a forgiving nature, despite his impatience. I will speak to him on your behalf when he returns, and hope that we can clear up this matter before any more damage is done."

"His lordship is away from home?" Mr. Hidgely asked, surprised.

"Yes, but I expect him back Saturday. Sunday morning, before services, I will have him speak with you, if that is acceptable."

"Quite acceptable, Lady Ledbetter." Mr. Hidgely rose when his hostess did. "Thank you. I'm sure I don't deserve your intervention, but I'm grateful for it."

"I think we will all be better for resolving this untenable situation," she replied. "Ledbetter is not his father, Mr. Hidgely. If you will come to understand that, I think the two of you will manage to rub along reasonably well together."

"I shall do my best, my lady."

Now if Ledbetter will do the same, Prudence thought, perhaps we can get on with our lives.

# Chapter Nineteen

Ledbetter felt a little guilty at not arriving back at Salston until Saturday afternoon. True, he had made it back in time for their dinner for the neighbors, but he really had intended to return on Friday to give his wife moral support, if nothing else, for her first attempt at entertaining in his ancestral home.

And he had looked forward to spending an enjoyable night in bed with her, too. The entire time he'd been away, her voice had whispered in his mind, "Can we do it again?" Her question both charmed and aroused him each time. If his mission had not been so important, he would have preferred to remain with Prudence and share with her the joys of the marriage bed.

But there was plenty of time for that, he had promised himself. They had a lifetime to spend together. Ledbetter was especially pleased with the thought, and with his perspicacity in choosing Prudence as his bride. He was so eager to see her on his return that he took the stairs two at a time, and burst into her sitting room with scarcely a knock on the door.

Tessie, who was attending to her mistress's hair, nearly dropped the hairbrush in her surprise at his precipitate entrance. Prudence merely stared at him. "William!" she exclaimed. "I was beginning to think I would have to entertain our guests by myself."

"I promised to be here in time for the dinner," he said, a little defensively. "I meant to be back sooner, but I was delayed."

"And was your trip successful?"

Ledbetter looked meaningfully at Tessie and said, "To some degree. I wonder if I might speak with you alone."

Tessie curtsied and slipped off, closing the door behind her. Ledbetter approached his wife almost hesitantly. "I would have been here yesterday, but there was someone I couldn't speak to until last night. And then this morning one of the traces had to be repaired before I could be on my way." He reached for her hands and lifted them to his lips. "Forgive me?"

"Of course," she said dismissively. But she did not meet his eyes.

"You really were afraid I wouldn't be back in time for the dinner?"

"I knew you intended to be back."

He could feel her struggle to greet him warmly. A smile rose to her lips, but it was a forced smile. She said, "Welcome home, William," but her voice held none of the richness he had so easily become accustomed to. There was even, he thought, a suspicion of moisture in her eyes.

What was this? Had she lost interest in him so easily? "Is everything all right?" he asked, troubled. "You're well?"

"Quite well, thank you."

"And Catherine and the baby?"

"So far as I know they're fine, too. They went home a few days ago, but I'm expecting her with Sir Geoffrey and his mother this evening."

"Good, good." Ledbetter tilted her chin up with his finger and bent to kiss her. "Will you wear your hair loose tonight, Prudence?"

"Tessie was trying to do something with it when you came in. I'd like the earrings to show. They're so beautiful."

He saw that she had the diamond necklace on, and the dangling earrings. "You don't want the tiara? It would look magnificent on you."

"Thank you, no. For a more formal occasion, perhaps. Tonight I intend to wear flowers in my hair."

"Ah." Ledbetter wasn't sure he cared for the idea of his wife wearing flowers in her hair, but he knew better than to say so, given the precarious nature of his connection with his bride at the moment. "Will it throw your schedule off if I sit and talk with you for a moment?"

"Not at all. But do allow enough time for yourself, William. You'll wish a bath and your valet has already taken great pains to lay out what he expects you to wear this evening."

"Has he, by God?" Ledbetter could feel his ire rising, but he shook off such a petty annoyance. What did it matter, after all? Balliot was much better at deciding what was an appropriate garment than Ledbetter himself. He pulled up one of the ridiculously fragile chairs that graced his wife's sitting room and sat down on it.

"Mr. Youngblood is actually a sort of cousin, it turns out," he told her.

"Yes, I know."

This was not the reaction Ledbetter had expected, and he frowned at her. "How could you possibly know?"

"I spoke with Mr. Newsom, and with Mr. Hidgely."

"I beg your pardon?"

"Mr. Newsom can understand perfectly well if you speak slowly and clearly to him. And he's been here such a long time that he seemed the natural person to ask about Mr. Youngblood."

"What can he possibly know of Mr. Youngblood?" Ledbetter demanded.

"Well, nothing for certain, of course, but he knew when he saw Mr. Youngblood in church that he must certainly be Francis's son. The curly hair, you understand."

"What are you talking about, Prudence?"

And so she told him. Ledbetter could scarcely credit what he heard. Here he had traveled for several days, meeting constant frustration and being obliged to cross the palms of every person in sight, and his wife had stayed home and disposed of the entire matter. He was not at all pleased with her promises to Mr. Hidgely, though he could understand the necessity for a reconciliation in that quarter.

"But he deliberately allowed my mother to believe that my father had been unfaithful to her. That he'd had a son with some other woman! The little toad."

"Yes," Prudence agreed, "but you must admit, William, that your father's behavior might easily provoke just such a reaction. And Mr. Hidgely has come to think of you as being a . . . somewhat similar person."

"The devil he has! When have I ever raised my voice to Hidgely, let alone call him a jackanapes? Not that I haven't wished to on occasion, you understand," he admitted, a trace of amusement in his voice. "You are a complete hand, Prudence. I can't believe you managed to unearth all that information—and from a deaf gardener and a self-righteous vicar. I should have stayed home."

"Yes, you should have," she said evenly. Then she waved him toward the door. "You need to get ready for our guests, William, and so do I. We'll talk more later."

"Indeed we will." He passed in front of her, allowing his hand to caress the line of her jaw. "But we'll do more than talk, I hope."

A blush suffused her cheeks, and she nodded.

"My adorable Prudence," he said. Then, with a regretful sigh, he took himself off.

As their guests gathered, Prudence did her best to put names with faces. She did not suffer from awkwardness in social situations, but rather enjoyed meeting new people. The fact that Ledbetter stood beside her, and that she was wearing those glorious diamonds, did nothing to detract from her enjoyment at being hostess in her new home.

For too many years she had been the eldest daughter, engaged but in limbo. Though she had seen to all the household duties at Colwyck, her mother was the lady of the manor. Her two sisters closest in age were impatient to have their turns in London, to find themselves potential husbands, but they had shown little interest in assisting Prudence in her efforts. So Prudence had learned how to run a household but had seldom received credit for her exertions.

Talk in the drawing room inexorably shifted to Mr. Youngblood. Prudence felt herself become alert to Ledbetter's replies to his guests' queries. She could see no sign of irritability; rather his openness about his probable relationship to the young man was admirable. He spoke with an almost offhand ease that brought a startled look from Sir Geoffrey. But it was Sir Geoffrey's mother who actually gave voice to her surprise.

"If I had known how much marriage would mellow you, William, I would have urged it on you a good deal sooner," she teased.

Her bluff manner did not seem to distress him. In fact Ledbetter offered her a mocking bow and said, "I had first to find a woman who refused to tolerate my rough ways, Lady Manning. Of course, she's only had a few days to

work on me. Who knows what a paragon I shall become
when we've been married for years?"

"I would dearly love to see the day you become a
paragon," the dowager Lady Manning said with a chuckle,
"but I don't expect I shall live that long."

"You wound me," Ledbetter retorted.

The butler arrived to announce that dinner was served.
This was the moment that Prudence had been waiting for.
Ledbetter insisted on escorting both the dowager and his
wife to the dining room. As they approached and a footman
threw open the door, Prudence heard the sharp intake of
breath beside her. "My God!" Ledbetter exclaimed.

The high-ceilinged room had indeed been transformed
into a garden. Not only were there rows of blooming flowers along the walls, but hanging baskets of them above. A
riot of color splashed everywhere—reds, yellows, blues,
purples. Plants peeked from behind the miniature hedges
and cascaded past a realistic rock wall. Down the center of
the table a vine of creeping Jenny twined, its yellow blossoms lushly accenting each place setting.

The candles in the chandelier twinkled gaily, like so
many sunbeams, Prudence thought. The effect was even
more stunning in the evening darkness than it had been in
the gloom of the afternoon. "Do you like it?" she asked
Ledbetter, unnecessarily.

"It's the most glorious thing I've ever seen," he said.
"How did you do it?"

"Well, it was Mr. Newsom who did it. He understood instantly what I had in mind."

Lady Manning, on Ledbetter's other side, said, "Oh,
William's mother would have loved this! How I wish she
could have seen it."

"It seemed a more fitting memorial than that great

organ," Prudence explained. "Everyone has mentioned how much she loved flowers and her gardens."

Behind them the other guests were making their way into the room, exclaiming at the spring garden which surrounded them. Catherine squeezed her hand, and Sir Geoffrey beamed his approval. Prudence flushed with delight at their pleasure. But it was the look on Ledbetter's face—of awe, and gratitude, and something more—which made her heart beat faster.

Prudence was exhausted. The evening had gone exceptionally well, but she had been relieved to see the last guest out the door. Ledbetter had turned to her then and caught her to him in an exuberant hug, saying, "That garden was magnificent. *You* were magnificent, Prudence. Lord, you must be fagged to death from all your efforts."

He had bent to whisper in her ear, "But I hope you will come to me tonight. Please say you will."

And she had promised that she would. When Tessie helped her to undress, excitedly relaying the pride of the Salston staff in the success of the spring garden and the dinner party, Prudence had smiled and nodded, but her thoughts were on her husband. She had won his admiration tonight, but had she earned his loyalty and consideration? Would he think twice before he up and left her alone at Salston another time? Prudence didn't wish to be merely a hostess to his guests, or even—amazing thought—a mother to his children. She wanted to be important to Ledbetter himself.

Perhaps that was asking too much, she thought as she removed every pin from her hair. She watched Tessie pull the brush carefully through her locks until they shone in the candlelight. This was the way he liked it, Prudence knew, in a wild nimbus around her head. "That will be all,

Tessie," she said. "Thank you for your help with the dinner. I'm so glad you agreed to come to me. Are you happy
here?"

"Oh, yes, my lady." The girl curtsied before heading toward the door, where she paused to say, "I'm going to learn
more about being a real dresser, ma'am. Mrs. Collins says
I'm to spend three hours a week with Fenner, as was the
dowager's dresser for thirty years."

She said this with something like reverence. "She's pensioned off now, but she lives in the village, and she'll teach
me about fashion and proper cleaning of garments, and all
she knows about caring for such a one as you. If it's agreeable with you that I go there, my lady."

"Why, of course it is. How splendid! Mrs. Collins must
be very taken with you to arrange for such a training."

"As to that," the girl replied, flushing, "she's been very
kind to me, but I think it is her wish to please you which
made her arrange it."

"In any case, I am grateful to her, and I shall tell her so
in the morning. Good night, Tessie."

"Good night, my lady."

Prudence sat alone for a few minutes, trying to collect
her thoughts. But her tired mind refused to cooperate, so
she sighed and rose to make her way across the hall. There
were things she needed to say to Ledbetter, matters of im-
portance to her, but she didn't seem to have the will to
bring them up, the courage to face him with them. Then
again, perhaps they were too insignificant, or too demanding, to be trotted out for his impatient inspection. She drew
a shaky breath as she knocked at his door and let herself
into his room.

He was seated in an armchair, the second volume of
*Emma* in his hands. He set the book down and reached a
hand out to her, so that she crossed the room to take it.

Then he pulled her gently onto his lap and nuzzled his face against her hair. "You must be very tired," he said.

"I'm afraid I am," she admitted. "And we have to get up early for church."

He groaned. "Where I will be forced to accept Hidgely's apology, and render one of my own."

"If you could see your way clear to doing it."

"Oh, I shan't have any trouble with that." He shrugged at her startled look. "It all seems rather unimportant now. There's something much more significant weighing on my mind."

"Whether Mr. Youngblood knew all along about the deception?"

He shook his head, drawing a finger along the line where the diamond necklace had rested all evening. "No, not that either. In time I'll discuss it with him and come to a decision about whether he deserves to be welcomed into the family. I don't actually hold with being estranged from one's cousins, whether they're legitimate or not."

"Then what is it that's of such concern to you?" she asked, puzzled.

"You are."

"Me?" Prudence felt a little alarmed. "Have I done something to displease you?"

"You know you haven't. But my guess is that I've done something that displeases you. I'm not quite sure what it was, though, Prudence. I fear I'm a little dull, and a little too self-absorbed, to have put my finger on what has upset you, so I can only beg that you will tell me."

Prudence swallowed painfully. "I'm not displeased with you, William."

"Now I fear that is not the whole truth, my dear, and I am accustomed to hearing the whole truth from you. There was that certain amount of reserve in you on my return. It would not have been there, I think, if I had not disappointed you in some way. It seemed more than just my being late in returning."

His finger dipped slightly to the cleft between her breasts, but his eyes remained on hers. Prudence cleared her throat, aware of a tension beginning to blossom in her body. "I . . . I have a strong aversion to being abandoned," she said at last. "I think I mentioned it to you before."

He cocked his head at her. "Yes, I think you did. But, my sweet, I merely left for a few days to investigate this problem. You knew I would be back very shortly. Surely you do not consider that abandonment."

When she said nothing, he tipped her chin up so she was forced to meet his gaze. "I don't understand. No doubt I'm being very dense, but you'll have to be a bit clearer."

"It felt like you were abandoning me," she said. "We'd only been married a few days. I know you married me because of the inheritance, but I didn't want other people to realize that . . . that you didn't care for me, that it was just a matter of convenience."

Ledbetter was frowning. "I thought we'd cleared this up the night before I left, Prudence. I do care for you, and I cared for you when I married you. Do you want me to confess all?"

"What is there to confess?"

"Mmm. A great deal, I suppose. When you became engaged to Porlonsby four years ago, I was acutely disappointed. I had thought I had some chance with you. You didn't seem entirely indifferent to me, though you did avoid any attempt I made to fix my interest with you."

Prudence nodded. "I was very aware of you, Will, but, as I have said, you frightened me. You were so . . . so fierce in your attentions."

"Only because of my attraction to you, Prudence. Even

then—" He sighed. "I told myself, when you chose Porlonsby, that my feelings would abate in time. Unfortunately, they didn't. So I miserably awaited word that you had married that stalwart young man. For several years I glanced through the marriage announcements in the paper, to see if that fateful day had arrived. But it never did."

"No, it never did," she said sadly.

A look of pain crossed his face. "Did you love him so much then, Prudence? Is there no chance that in time you will come to hold me in regard?"

"Oh, Will, there is so much I too should confess to you." She laid her cheek against his, her head bowed. "I suppose I loved Allen. Certainly I felt safe with him, and treasured. He was so very *kind* to me."

"I don't understand why he didn't return to marry you," Ledbetter said softly. "How could he have not hastened back at the first opportunity?"

"Yes, that is what I have wondered all these years," she admitted, her face still pressed against his. "He accumulated quite a fortune, as you have seen for yourself, William. Surely he could have returned after a year or two, with less, but sufficient to make marriage possible."

She could feel the tears start, as they had many times over the last years. As they spilled over and rolled down her cheeks, she pulled back from Ledbetter so that he wouldn't feel them. But he cradled her in his arms, his hand pressing her head against his shoulder. "Cry, then," he whispered. "Mourn him properly, my love. Time will ease that pain."

Prudence wiped angrily at the tears. "It's not for love of him that I cry, Will. I would that it were. It is the awful humiliation I've felt at being abandoned by him. He *could* have come back; he *could* have married me. In truth, he chose not to."

"But why?"

"I don't know. He never explained. He never said he wasn't coming back. Year after year passed and I was left to put a brave face on my 'engagement.' My sisters were impatient for me to wed, my parents began to grow suspicious of Allen's intentions. He could not cry off, of course."

"No, of course not."

"So I wrote, offering to do so myself. Oh, a very long time ago. He never responded to that letter. It was as if I'd never written. So I wrote again, and again. But, though he wrote, he never addressed that issue. I was at my wit's end when word of his death reached me. A local epidemic of cholera had claimed his life. His will, leaving me all of his property, had been made at the time of his departure for India. I will never know why he didn't return."

"But you suspect—what?"

Prudence drew a shaky breath. "Oh, that he fell in love there, I suppose. Or even married, and was ashamed to tell me. Or, simply that he found he had no real attachment to me, once he was far away. I would have gone to India. I suggested that, too, but he did not reply."

Her tears had dried now. In fact, she felt a great deal better, having told him of her impossible situation regarding Porlonsby. She smiled a little mistily, saying, "I'm afraid that's why your leaving me made me feel abandoned, Will. Foolish of me, perhaps, but I could not bear feeling such humiliation again."

"I'm sorry, Prudence. It was thoughtless of me. And I didn't even *want* to leave you," he admitted, rueful. "Nor did I have to leave to solve this ludicrous puzzle, as it turns out."

He bent to kiss her, his lips lingering on hers. "The love I felt for you in London was a pale thing compared with what I feel tonight, Prudence. Every day since we've been married my affection for you has grown. I love what a splendid woman you are—how generous and clever and kind you are. And I'm grateful that I feel myself a better man just being with you. I'm afraid you won't agree with me, since I have been so careless of your sensibilities, but believe me that I want nothing more than to make you happy."

"You *do* make me happy, Will," she said, feeling the tears prick at her eyes once more. "It is I who have been foolish beyond permission. If I had not feared your virility when first we met, we might have come to an agreement years ago."

"Let's assume this is the way it was meant to be, and not suffer from regrets, my love. We were meant to be older, and wiser, when we came together."

"I've been thinking a great deal about our coming to-gether," she said, her cheeks flushing. "You mustn't think that our physical intimacy is the only reason that I love you, though. I knew as soon as you showed up at Colwyck that my attraction to you in London had not been illusory. Like you, even the pressures on me would not have in-duced me to marry someone I did not wish to marry."

"With your inheritance as a dowry, you could have had your pick of any number of eligible gentlemen."

Prudence shrugged. "Possibly. Thank heaven you hap-pened to be at the Rightons'."

Ledbetter laughed. "I didn't *happen* to be there, Pru-dence. Since I had learned of your fiancé's demise, I'd an-gled for a way to bring myself to your notice again. And not because of your inheritance."

"Did you?" His bride sighed. "I think perhaps it is time you brought yourself to my notice again, Will. There are parts of me that feel a little abandoned just now. They wonder when you plan to attend to them."

"Ah, I stand corrected, my lady." Ledbetter's hand came to cup the swell of her breast. "Is this one of those parts?"

"Yes," she said, "but there are others."

"In that case, I think we had best adjourn to my bed. If it pleases your ladyship."

"It pleases me very much."

So Ledbetter lifted her in his arms and carried her across the room to their marriage bed, where he managed in short order to allay any fears that might have disturbed his new bride's complete and total happiness.